USA *TODAY* BESTSELLING AUTHOR

Dale Mayer

TERKEL'S TEAM SERIES
TERKEL'S TWIST

BOOK 08

TERKEL'S TWIST: TERKEL'S TEAM, BOOK 8
Beverly Dale Mayer
Valley Publishing Ltd.

ISBN-13: 978-1-773365-30-5
Print Edition

Books in This Series:

About This Book

Welcome to a brand-new series from *USA Today* best-selling author Dale Mayer, where dark-ops SEALs have special senses and skills, needed to solve intrigue, betrayal, and ... murder. A series with all the elements you've come to love, plus so much more, ... including psychics!

In advance of another major attack, Terk races to Levi's compound in Texas, where Terk finally gets to meet Celia, the woman carrying his child. Thankfully he arrives in time to protect his friends and *new* family from another attack, but he's determined to get to the end of this nightmare that tried to earlier destroy his team.

Finally meeting this stranger—whose child Celia may be carrying—how could she not be suspicious? But after meeting Terk, she believes he had nothing to do with her pregnancy. Only after some deep conversations, as they peel layer from layer, do possible answers surface.

When the pieces finally come together into the most probably theory, Terk realizes how simple this whole mess really is. But solving it? ... That's a whole different story.

PROLOGUE

THE TRIP TO Texas was brutal. The flight long, noisy, and tedious, when so much in Terk's life was on hold. He'd sent out probes, checking on everyone multiple times, and everyone was fine. Even with that reassurance it was hard for him to relax.

While his brother was at his side, a rare moment for the two of them, it was hard knowing what was coming and what they'd left behind.

"Have you told them where we are?" Merk asked him.

Terk nodded. "Yes, but I've also slowed the energy going to them, so I'll call them when we land."

Merk shook his head but remained silent; then out of the blue, he said, "You know that, even though I'm used to this, it still sounds bizarre what you're saying."

Not much Terk could say to that. His brother had long been his biggest supporter, but that adaptation couldn't have been easy. Terk had often wondered if there was something Merk couldn't tap into or ignored either willfully or subconsciously all these years. In Terk's case, his extra senses dominated. Ignoring them wasn't even possible.

"What are you and your team going to do when this is over?" Merk murmured, looking out the plane window. "We're almost there."

"I know, and I've spent much of this flight resting, letting the energy flow in the direction it needs to, and it heads to England every time."

Merk stared at him sharply. "As in a permanent location? As in the entire team or just yourself?"

"Yes, as to location and as in the whole team, including all the new members."

"And Celia?"

That was a question Terk couldn't answer. No one could at this stage. He could see bits and pieces, images that were both dark and intense, yet sprinkled in between softer ones. He knew Celia was important, but the jury was out as to whether she was on the plus side or the minus side. Terk could only hope that, given what he did know, she wasn't involved in the making of this nightmare. If she was, good luck keeping his son away from him. If she wasn't involved in that way, then Terk knew the future would get very interesting, very soon.

The seat belt sign kicked on.

Merk looked over at him and smiled. "You ready? To meet Celia? To see what the hell is going on at this end?"

"Always," Terk murmured, looking at the approaching runway. "And more than ready to end this. Whatever the hell *this* is …"

CHAPTER 1

TERKEL ARMAND SLIPPED out of the truck and studied the huge concrete structure that rose in front of him. Multiple vehicles were parked around them, but the energy seemed off. "The compound appears empty."

At that, Merk sucked in a heavy breath. "Yeah." He nodded, but his expression was worried. "They could be hiding in a lot of places around here. It doesn't have to be bad news."

"No, I'm not sure it's bad news yet," Terk replied, "but something is odd about it."

"Odd how? Do you want to define that a little better?"

"Is Katina here?"

"No, she's on a trip to California," he admitted. "It's one of the reasons why I came to help you."

At that, Terk's lips twitched. "What? She didn't ask to come with you?"

"She's not used to this madness. It would have created more problems than it solved."

"Because of me?"

"You and I are very close, always have been. When you need help, I'm there. She knows that."

Merk had always done so, right from the beginning. Terk nodded calmly. Right now, more trouble than he cared to acknowledge was up ahead. He just wasn't certain when it was coming or in what form. "I'm definitely getting an odd reading from the compound."

"You want to go through the back way?"

"No. … I think, if we go any other way than straight through the front, it'll look odd."

"I'd rather look odd and still be alive," Merk noted calmly.

"Maybe, but it's not that kind of an oddness."

Merk shrugged. "I trust you. Let's go." Together they walked up to the garage entrance.

"Gates are closed. Alarm systems are running still, so why am I getting a sense of emptiness?" Terk was bewildered.

"Our new security? Something you haven't come up against?"

"Possibly." Terk glanced over at his brother.

"Have you got something?" Merk asked him.

"No, I am not getting much from out here, and I'm not at my best. No strange heat signatures."

"We have a new technology that closes down heat recognition," Merk replied, with a nod.

"I wondered as much," Terk murmured. As they walked up to the compound, both of them with weapons in hand, Merk took the lead and unlocked the inner gate to let them in.

Terk remained confused, and his energy was all over the place. "Still feels weird."

"*Weird* is pretty normal in your world, so I can't dispute that," Merk replied. "What about your own personal security setup? I am sure you did something in the ethers or whatever to make sure that we were safe too."

"I did. … Yet still something's affecting that."

"Interesting. So take a wild guess. Humor me."

"I can't. I don't know," Terk replied in frustration. As they walked forward a few steps, he stopped. "Something else has shifted."

At that, the door in front of them opened casually. They both looked up in unison, and there she was. Ice. Standing tall and strong in front of them and ... smiling.

Merk raced forward to her. "We weren't sure what the hell we were sensing, but definitely something was off. Even Terk wasn't sure."

"Yeah." She shrugged. "We'll have to talk about that, Terk."

He frowned at her. "About what?"

She lowered her voice. "You tell me. After all, you've had a chance to see the signatures."

"Definitely some disrupting energy is here that I didn't put in place." Terk nodded.

"I'm getting that too," she stated. "That makes better sense. It's good to have you here."

He walked over, gave her a big hug. "Thank you—for everything."

"You're welcome." Ice smiled. "By the way, she's a sweetheart."

He laughed. "That's good to know because we have some difficult news to deal with right now."

"The biggest of which is what?" she asked, as she closed the door behind them. "What the hell's going on, and how close are we to bringing this to an end?"

Terk caught movement at another door, and he quickly turned to see Levi. He relaxed a bit, seeing him walk toward him, with a big grin on his face. The two men exchanged a hard hug.

"It's good to see you," Levi greeted him. "Glad you brought Merk back with you."

Terk smiled, loving the absolute acceptance he always got from these guys. He knew part of it was the years working with his brother and the number of times Terk had called in to warn them about something that would go crazy on them. They had a long history of helping each other in shitstorms that they couldn't possibly see for themselves.

"It is good to see you guys." Terk smiled. "It's been a rather tough couple months."

"You think?" Merk quipped. "You do realize both the DGSE and MI6 were gunning for you to get out of their respective countries?"

"I try hard not to think about it, and I won't give them a chance to interfere with my work. The DGSE doesn't need to worry, as we only visit France from time to time. Now MI6 on the other hand … On another topic, I warned my team to stay in place, but I'm afraid they are pretty adamant about being on the spot and seeing this thing through." Terk looked over at Levi and saw his lips twitch, then asked forcefully, "They already contacted you, didn't they?"

Levi nodded. "Of course. I get that you think that they don't need to come to your aid, but think about it from their perspective. They aren't willing to let you get into trouble without them."

"I was hoping *not* to get into trouble."

"Yeah, right. And how's that been working out for you?" Levi asked.

Terk rolled his eyes at his old friend. "Not very well lately. Talk about a shitstorm."

"Exactly," Levi agreed, "but that's okay. We're here to help."

"You've already helped a lot. I don't want you, … any of you, to get into any more trouble than you already are."

Levi laughed. "It'll just get uglier."

"It always gets ugly before it gets better."

"And this is what we do, Terk."

"Sure, but you also have a lot of people here to look after."

"And you've added to that," Levi pointed out calmly, not pulling any punches.

"I know. I didn't know anything about her, except that she was on the way here, and I'm sorry for that," Terk said. "I didn't have any idea what was happening, until all of a sudden she was *there*."

Immediately a question came from the inner doorway. "She?"

He turned, as an obviously pregnant woman stepped into the big kitchen.

Celia. Instantly her energy—hesitant yet compelled by something she might not even understand—darted toward him. An energy glowing with a second presence, the baby. His baby. Bemused, he could only watch in fascination. He saw her, felt her, and *knew* what she was to him. He stepped forward and held out his hand. "Hello, I am Terk."

She nodded calmly but ignored his hand. "About time you got here."

His eyebrows shot up. He pulled back his hand. "What does that mean?"

She gave him an exasperated look. "Let's not play games. Obviously you know more about this than you're letting on." She indicated the bump that she carried.

"Actually I don't," he said immediately, "and, for that, I'm sorry. I really wish I did know more."

It was her turn for her eyebrows to rise. "What about all of these last many weeks in England?"

"*That* I know about," he admitted, "and, yes, I knew of your existence and when you arrived at this place, but that is the extent of it. We're still trying to get to the bottom of your story. We have a lot of the pieces now but more gaps."

"Okay"—she took a deep breath—"so why are you here then?"

He hesitated for a split second. "Because I believe an attack is imminent, and I wanted to be here to do what I could do to stop it."

"How imminent?" she asked, her eyes going wide, as she took in the expressions on the other people's faces.

"I was half-expecting that it had already happened, when I sensed the off security here."

"Off security?" she asked in a low voice. "Do you want to explain that?"

"Not right now." He studied her, wondering if she understood she was the one putting out the defensive energy bristling in the room. "How are you feeling?"

"Better*ish*. I mean, nothing like waking up from a coma to find that you're ... halfway through a pregnancy you know nothing about, while wired up to explosives and stumbling on a backroad, with no memory as to how I got there."

"Do you want to explain the pregnancy?"

She snorted. "No, I don't. And definitely not to you."

"Why definitely not to me?"

"Because, according to Ice, you seem to think it's yours, and I can tell you right now, it's not."

"Well, I won't argue with you. Besides DNA will prove it, one way or the other."

"Exactly. Glad we agree on that at least, and, by the way, that's not happening until my son is born."

He knew that her getting more upset wouldn't benefit anybody. He turned to face Ice. "Have you got a game plan?"

Her beautiful features twisted in a wry smile. "Somewhat. Let's go get coffee and maybe get you some food. Then we can go over it."

"That would be nice." Terk rotated his neck ever-so-slowly and gently widened his senses. When he came into a place like this, with many different people living and working here, it was always really hard to hold back the surge of energy around the compound. With his brother, Terk didn't have to do it on account of his similarity and familiarity. As twins, their energy was damn near the same. But, with so many different personalities here, their energy was rampant.

As Terk followed Ice, Merk grabbed his arm to pull him back slightly. "So, do you know her?" he asked.

Terk immediately shook his head. "No, and I told you that from the beginning."

"Jesus."

Terk looked at him and said, "It's mine." And, with that declaration, not anything anybody could say. When Terk was adamant, he was adamant. Like he'd said, the DNA would prove it out, but still …

"Do you think this was deliberate?" Merk muttered, as they walked forward. "Your child, I mean. Not just anyone's."

"I can't help but think that it was. I just don't understand how it came to be. According to Yousef, it was planned."

As they walked into the big dining room, Alfred bustled from the kitchen. A smile broke out on his face as he looked at Terk. "There you are. Now I can stop worrying about you."

"You were worried about me?" Terk asked in confusion.

"Of course. This is a very difficult time for you, so it's very important that you have all the support you need." And, with that said, Alfred frowned at the sideboard and added, "I'll go get the cinnamon buns. I'll be right back." He disappeared into the adjoining room.

At that abrupt declaration and even faster departure, Levi looked over at Ice. "So Terk gets cinnamon buns? I've been asking for cinnamon buns for days."

Ice burst out laughing. "I think you'll survive. Besides, I'm pretty sure you had some just a few days ago."

"But that was a few days ago," Levi argued. "Do you have any idea how much this crew eats?"

"Speaking of which," Terk added, as he stopped at the entrance to the dining room, his senses slowly spreading farther, "the place is almost empty."

"It is," Levi agreed. "Threats of an imminent attack have us setting priorities and removing many of the partners—not to mention children—from the compound. And, of course, that means sending several of the men along with them. We also have others of the team off on jobs," Levi added. "It's become a bit of a scheduling nightmare. We're always struggling for new members."

"Well, I guess that's a good thing."

"Maybe." Levi glanced at Terk. "Of course sometimes personal crises come up."

"It's not as if Merk would give us a chance to say no," Ice chipped in, with a bright smile.

"And it would never be an issue because you are family too, Terk," Levi said calmly.

It was such an odd, yet welcome thing. He and Merk had worked separately for a very long time, but once Merk had hooked up with Levi and Ice, Terk had automatically been included in the group, like an extended part of the family you didn't know was there but accepted anyway. And it was rather nice.

Terk smiled at Ice, then walked over to give her a big hug and whispered, "Are you looking forward to your daughter? It won't be just yet ..." He paused, tilted his head, and a date popped in his mind. He whispered it against her temple.

Ice's eyes widened. "What?"

He chuckled. "I can't help what I learn. Such as the cycle of life and all."

At that, Levi turned and looked at the two of them. "What did he say to you?"

"I'm not saying a word," she murmured, a tiny smile at the corner of her lips.

"Damn it, Terk," Levi growled, shooting him a look, before turning to look at Ice. "No secrets. Remember that?"

"No secrets, but that doesn't mean there isn't a need for discretion." Then she turned, looked at the others, and added, "Bailey's not here. It's just Alfred in the kitchen. So it'll be a little less fancy."

"I don't need fancy," Terk replied.

At that, Alfred returned with a big tray of cinnamon buns. "You forgot to mention that Celia's been in the kitchen helping me too." Alfred beamed. "I keep trying to get her out of there, but she won't listen."

"None of you ever listen," Levi growled again. "We do

the best we can do, but it's like shepherding goats."

"I think the phrase is *sheep*." Celia walked in calmly, carrying a stack of plates, and put them on the sideboard. Terk sat in the closest chair.

"Well, sheep at least follow along blindly," Levi snorted. "Trying to get you guys to do anything is impossible."

"That's because we know that you're doing it to get us out of the way." Celia picked up a plate and plunked a large cinnamon bun on it, then walked over and put it down in front of Terk. Then she went back and grabbed another plate and did the same for Merk. When she went back a third time, Terk looked over at Levi. "See? You might get one after all."

"I'll probably have to get it myself though." He growled yet again.

He watched as the cinnamon buns quickly got divvied up. But, before he could say anything, Ice walked over and put a large plate down in front of him, with two cinnamon buns. "Just in case you really feel like we did you wrong," she murmured.

He glared at her. "You know these are cinnamon buns, right?"

"Yep, I sure do." She gave a bright chuckle. "I also know that you get them all the time."

"Sure, but I haven't had one in a while, at least a couple days." He rubbed his hands together, looking at the plate with delight.

Terk watched the byplay, a smile on his face. It was so lovely to see them together. For the longest time, he thought a romantic partnership wasn't something they could manage long-term, so their energy sliding along in a cozy pairing made his heart smile. His own intuition warned him that those two strong-willed and dominant people in a relationship would always be a challenge. Yet they were still handling everything pretty well.

So maybe challenges themselves weren't bad after all. And, for these two, maybe that was what really made things work for them. Terk didn't say it out loud, but they had restored his faith in humanity, and somehow they seemed to have done that for a lot of people.

They were the first couple to marry and to have children in their circle of professionals, and, because they had survived, they were now surrounded by many other happy couples. The energy flowing easily from Levi and Ice then raised the energies of everyone in the vicinity, which in turn made the collective energy vibrate at a higher level, thus repeating the cycle. "How many weddings do you have scheduled this year?" Terk asked.

Ice rolled her eyes. "There have been requests for quite a few actually."

The little bit of hesitation in Ice's words and mannerisms had Terk eyeing her expectantly.

She added, "But some people have family who can't come. Well, that and the security risks. And others just wanted to have a quiet affair, and then, of course, some wanted to go to Vegas."

Merk snorted at that, but he kept his head down and buried in the cinnamon bun. "Ceremony is just that, ceremony," he stated. "It really has nothing at all to do with the life that you live."

"That's our opinion too," Ice agreed, "but, for some people, there's a reverence to the pomp that helps solidify the seriousness of a promise made. And, in your case"—she looked at Merk—"you never really got a divorce."

13

"Well, we did, but I guess we didn't ..." He shrugged, gave Ice a gentle smile. "Who knew that, even drunk, I could pick out the best partner."

At that, Ice laughed. "And apparently it was reciprocal."

"Absolutely." The conversation was light and gentle for the rest of the time, as Terk scarfed down the cinnamon bun, even as he kept one eye on Celia.

As soon as his plate was empty, he pushed it back and said, "We need to talk, Ice. What are the plans?"

"Yep," Ice agreed, "that's number one," as she looked at the tablet in her hand. "Terk, update us. What are we facing?"

With that, Terk quickly went over the news from the last scenario.

"Should we expect the rest of your team to come?" she asked. "Or just half of them?"

"I tried hard to keep them out of it. So I don't know. There have been so many attempts on their lives already, I didn't really want them all in the same place, while another attack is happening."

"That's what being a leader is all about," Levi noted calmly. "We have a lot of people trying to get involved in this too." He frowned and continued. "I know you don't like that idea, but we have to do something in order to keep the information flowing."

"Are you sure you guys don't want to take off and just let Merk and me handle it?"

"Not happening," Ice stated, her voice cool. "This is our home. They brought us into this by sending Celia here. And, if I haven't said it to you before, I'm staying."

"Thank you very much for letting me come in. And ... for staying," Celia added.

"You're welcome," Ice replied gently. "When shit hits the fan, this is the stuff we do. So far, since your arrival, we have had no attacks on our compound … yet." Ice stared at Terk.

"No, but there will be."

"When?" she asked almost immediately.

"Forty-two hours at best."

That answer was so precise, her eyebrows went up. She wrote it down, then checked the wall clock immediately.

"Now that's a very specific figure."

"It is. And accurate, as near as I can tell you at this point."

"Good, that gives us time to prepare." Ice looked over at Levi. "That's shorter than we thought but maybe better than we deserve. We've got a lot of security plans in place because we've been expecting this—and we do have a skeleton crew of us here."

Terk nodded. "Is Stone around?"

"Yes, Stone is definitely here." She smiled.

"And I presume the satellite is up and running?" Terk asked them.

"Always," Levi said, stepping in. "We have all the entrances and exits covered. We've enlarged our coverage area a bit, and we've got hidden cameras around, approaching the area. I've got offers going to buy a few more acres around our place, so we can expand our security a bit farther," he shared, "but, so far, I haven't managed to get any bites yet."

"That would be a good move." Terk stared off in the distance. "This won't be the only attack at your place."

"Nope, it's not the first and sure won't be the last," Levi agreed. "Considering that families are expanding here, it's not a bad idea to continue to expand our holdings as well."

"Did you consider buying one of the properties next over?" Terk asked. "It's coming up for sale."

"Which one?" Ice looked at him.

Terk frowned, got up, and moved to the map in the middle of the dining room table. Then slowly turning the map, Terk pointed with his finger. "That one."

"MacGyver's place," Ice noted.

"Yes, that's the name."

"Any idea why he's selling?"

"He's got cancer. The family won't want to keep it after he's gone, so he'll sell it first."

At that, Levi got up and walked out of the room. Ice nodded. "He's good friends with MacGyver."

"Sorry but also good. It's perfect timing too."

"That would be great, if we can come to an agreeable price," Ice said.

"He's got a large property."

"Yes, he does. Quite a few acres."

"That would be a very helpful holding to have," Terk added.

"Agreed." She hesitated. "Terk, is there anything else you've intuitively picked up on that we should know?"

"I'm not sure. Everything feels odd here."

"Well, take some time to adjust." Then she turned her attention to Celia, looking over at her keenly. "Are you feeling okay? Do you need to lie down?"

Celia waved her hand. "I'll be fine. This is pretty fascinating to watch. Do you always believe what he says?"

"Always."

Terk looked at her. "Are you ready to tell me what happened to you?"

"More than what Ice already told you?"

"While I did hear some things from Ice, I find that it's always better to hear things in someone's own words."

"Well, I don't remember very much," Celia stated flatly.

He frowned. "Were you drugged, do you think?" he asked, then turned to look at Ice.

"Yes, she did have quite a cocktail in her system, when we brought her into the compound, and we've been doing as much as we can to get that cleaned out. We have already cleared some of the issues, but obviously stress is a huge factor. Plus, being pregnant limited our treatment options."

"Of course," he murmured. He studied Celia intently.

She shifted uneasily, stiffening, then she glared at him. "Don't look at me like that," she snapped. "I haven't done anything."

"Do you have any foreign connections?"

She looked like she had been struck by a thousand watts. "Why would you even ask that?"

"Where were you six, seven months ago?"

She flushed, then glared again.

He just gave her that flat stare. He knew when people were hiding something, and, although she had every right to be upset over what had happened, he had to be sure nothing was hidden from him. Trust had to work both ways.

"I was in London at the time."

At that, he sat back. "Doing what?"

Celia looked at Merk and then Ice. When her gaze landed on Terk, again a flash of hostility crossed her face. She turned her head. "I was there for an interview."

"And then what?" he asked, his gaze unwavering.

"I'm not exactly sure. I did a bunch of work in England," she said thoughtfully. "And then I traveled to France. ... Nothing seemed to be any different or out of ordinary. Nothing seemed to be difficult. It was all good. Normal—until I was kidnapped."

"When did you realize you were pregnant?"

"When I woke up here. I don't think I realized it even while I was walking here. As far as Ice could tell, I'm approximately six months along." Her glare upped in wattage. "And, no, I don't know how this child was conceived or what happened afterward."

He could see her pain, the fear of finding out the truth of what happened to her. ... "Zero signs?"

"This entire conversation is making me uncomfortable."

"That's fine." He continued to study her. "You can blame me all you want. But that doesn't change the fact that you're carrying my child and that I want to know exactly how that happened and how you are connected to these attacks."

"I'm not. I've got nothing to do with it." She stood and held her belly protectively. Her words were literally venom now, and her eyes shot daggers. "And it's not your child. Maybe you should explain to me why you think it is and how I got that way?"

CELIA JUST WANTED to get away. There was almost a magnetic spell around that man, but he was also dangerous as hell. Her hands cradled her belly. While she waited on Terk to respond, she repeated the mantra in her head, *We'll be fine*, a mantra that she had been working on ever since she found out the crazy turn her life had taken. *We'll get through this. We'll be fine.*

Though, in reality, she wasn't sure how she was ever

supposed to be fine, given this nightmare she was in. She had hoped that, when she saw Terk, she would recognize him and would have remembered something about him and that somehow this would all begin to make sense.

But there wasn't anything. Nothing at all.

How was it even possible? He said he was the father of her child, but she could only look at him suspiciously because she'd never met him before. So how had he impregnated her? She could only imagine the ways such an event could have come about. None of them filled her with joy, nor gave her any measure of comfort. She had absolutely no idea who the father of her child was because she had no way of knowing when or how she got pregnant in the first place. A fact that just blew her away.

"So you'll ask me questions but not answer mine?" Celia asked Terk.

She didn't live in a world of casual relationships, where people routinely had unprotected sex and got pregnant out of the blue like that. She was always extremely careful, and her last breakup had been just ugly enough that she wasn't even close to being interested in another relationship and hadn't been for a long time. Yet she'd been kidnapped, held captive, impregnated, wired up with C-4, and released in an unknown rural area.

When?

Where?

And most certainly, why?

But she also knew this world was pretty messed up, and all kinds of people were out there. People who didn't give a crap and had ulterior motives, which also made her very suspicious of everything and everyone. Including *him*.

The bottom line was that this mess was not what she

wanted in any way, shape, or form. She needed to find the answers, or she would never be safe. To have Terk so adamant about her baby's paternity had sent her world into a tailspin.

She turned, left the dining room. She only stopped at the kitchen door, when, out of the corner of her eye, Alfred stepped out and handed her a cup of soothing tea. She smiled out of habit. "I'm really not an invalid. You know that, right?"

"I know you're not an invalid," Alfred stated, "but this meeting was always going to be stressful."

"Right from the beginning."

"So, if there's anything we can do to make it easier, we should."

"Why does everybody think it's his child?" she murmured.

"I don't know, but Terk is …" Alfred stopped abruptly, thinking about how much to tell her, then frowned, deciding it best to leave it to the others to tell her. "Let's just say, … Terk knows stuff."

She stared at him. "Knows what stuff? And why haven't I heard about it?"

"You have. People have mentioned it, yet you've barely scratched the surface of the crazy. The details are not mine to tell you, and that's probably how everyone feels around here." He shrugged. "It's just that nobody's come out and said anything clearly yet. But that conversation where he knew about the neighbor having cancer and it being the right time to buy real estate? Well, that's prime Terk for you."

"Maybe," she murmured, "but here I am, carrying a child, … six months' pregnant. Yet everybody else seems to know something about it that I don't. I didn't even know I was pregnant, until I woke up here."

Alfred immediately patted her shoulder gently. "Honestly, this has been something Terk has been trying to deal with during the same time as well."

"Right." Celia took a deep breath. "I just wish he didn't think I was to blame."

At that, his voice sounded from behind her. "As soon as I know you're not to blame, then I'll be fine with it. In the meantime, from my perspective, it looks very suspicious."

She turned and glared at him. "Well, from my perspective, you don't look that believable either."

His eyebrows shot up. "What does that mean?"

"I don't know you. I don't know who the father of my child is. I wasn't expecting to be pregnant, and believe me. I feel very leery of all males right now. To think that I'm in this position and have no conscious memory of how I got here is terrifying."

"Yet earlier you said I was not the father."

"What?"

"Right out in the hall, you very specifically said, I was not the father of this child. Why did you say that?"

"Because I don't know you. It's not possible. It can't be. And, if it is possible, then I don't trust you."

"That I can understand," he agreed. "I can tell you, however, I had nothing to do with it. I did not rape you. I didn't force myself on you in any way. I haven't donated to a sperm bank. Until all this started, I had no knowledge of the existence of a child—or of you for that matter."

She sagged under his revelations. "Well, at least that's plain talk."

"I do find plain talk works the best," he noted, "in my world anyway."

She nodded slowly. "Nothing makes any sense right now."

"That is often the way this kind of thing happens," he murmured. "I'm very sorry that you're in this situation. It's definitely something I would not have wanted for anybody. It's certainly not something I thought would happen personally in my own life," he stated, sounding resigned.

"Are you angry about the pregnancy?"

"I'm scared," she stated bluntly. "I'm in an ugly scenario of having lost months of my life. You're making claims that it's your child, and, all the while, I don't have the slightest idea how I even got into this situation. Yet at the same time, my maternal instincts have already kicked in, and I don't want anything to happen to my child."

He smiled, although it wasn't enough to hide the jet lag.

And something about that tilt of his lips made her realize just how tired he was and how reasonable he was trying to be.

He added, "Believe me. I don't want anything to happen to him either."

"Him?"

"Him." Terk nodded. "Male energy."

"Are you ever wrong?"

A ghost of a smile crossed his lips. "Not that I can remember."

She groaned, as she stared at him. Just because she had come to the same instinctive answer herself didn't help. She also thought she knew something else that she had no intention of sharing at this time. "If, for the moment, we consider the fact that you aren't wrong, I don't even want to think about *how?*" she asked, scared and edging away from him. "Somehow we—you and I—produced a fetus that neither of us knew about?"

He nodded slowly, then that grin peeped out. "Not in the fun way either."

She flushed brilliantly. "*Great.*"

He shrugged under a dark cloud of uncertainty. "Humor tends to make some of these situations a bit easier, reducing the stress."

"Oh, I get it," she muttered, "but, if we didn't ... hook up, and you didn't rape me ..."

Terk immediately interjected, "I assure you, I did neither. I was in Paris and England about the same time frames as you were," he shared. "I was knocked unconscious, totally lights out, in an attack about seven months ago. I'm just wondering if that's when my sperm was harvested. And believe me. That makes me feel *very* violated too."

"Is that even possible?" she asked.

He shrugged. "I was unconscious for several days. I came out of it with some pretty ugly dreams that I never could explain. So I don't have any explanation for that, but I wonder if that's potentially what I was processing."

"That would be ..." She stopped and shook her head. "I'm not even sure what that would be."

"Exactly," he murmured. "The planning for this"—he pointed at her bump, as politely as he could without being offensive—"was obviously done a long time ago." He paused. "Is it possible that you are an innocent victim?" he finally asked out loud.

"Possible?" she repeated, glaring at him. "Wow, thanks a lot for that."

"What do you want me to say? I've just met you, and I'm having to take a look at who you are," he explained. "It will obviously take me a little bit of time to adjust."

"You and me both." She stared past him. "Then add to that the fact that you consider this your child."

"It *is* my child," he stated firmly, with absolutely zero uncertainty.

"How can you be so sure?" she cried out. "For all you know, whatever they did to me didn't take right away, and they did it twice or three different times," she noted bitterly.

Understanding filled his gaze, as he nodded. "And I could say the same thing."

She didn't want to accept that but knew he was right. "Okay, so it's possible that we're both victims," she agreed, with difficulty. "As much as I don't even want to think about being a victim, I'm not sure that any other explanation is applicable at this point in time."

"So, if we'll agree that it's quite possible that we're both victims," Terk began, "then it would be nice if you would give me that leeway and accept that I didn't do anything to you."

She took a deep breath. "Maybe. You can bet that everybody here has been singing your praises since I first showed up. What the hell is that all about?"

CHAPTER 2

"**W**ELL, FIRST, I was really hoping that you could help explain everything to me," Terk noted, with no humor in his countenance.

She shook her head. "I really can't because I honestly don't know what happened. When I woke up, I was already strapped up with C-4. ... I was dropped off on this country road and told to walk up to this house or else. No, I didn't know the men, and they wore full head masks. It was a white van, but that's all I know. Ice will confirm the state I was in when I arrived."

"What was the first thing you remember?"

She frowned. "Ice has been asking me that, but I just have this big blank in my head from before."

"It's important, so we can track your movements. That's why I came over here, to meet with you and to solve this mystery."

"And to protect the compound?"

"I wouldn't insult Levi and Ice like that," he said. "They do very well here, and they're real pros. I know they've got everything under control."

Her gaze widened. "Is it that simple to you?"

He looked at her. "I don't know that anything is simple, but that part is fairly simple, yes."

She shook her head. "They'll be under attack. Don't you

DALE MAYER

want to help?"

"Of course, if I'm here, I would like—scratch that—I would love to help." He laughed. "But, at the same time, in order for this attack to either never take place or to be the last one, we need to deal with this."

"Right," she murmured. Then she took a deep breath. "Sorry, I … Your presence appears to have upset me."

"You knew I was coming?" he asked, with that intense gaze directed at her.

"Of course I did," she stated, "but I figured that, once you saw me, you wouldn't recognize me and would then understand that I wasn't carrying your child. I thought it would be a simple case of mistaken identity."

"It isn't. So?"

At that, she burst out laughing. "Oh, good God, I honestly appreciate the fact that you are so prosaic about it because I've been going around in circles on it. I've answered as many questions as I possibly could all this time, but I've yet to get any answers."

"We'll get them," he stated, his voice calm and reassuring, "but I do need to track your history, as much as we can."

"I'm sure that Ice has already done that and handed it off to you."

"And yet none of that is the same as hearing it firsthand."

She glared at him. "You know that this is not terribly easy to talk about."

"No, it definitely isn't." He showed his palms. "I'm just trying to get to the bottom of it. Remember. If we're both victims, then we both need to figure out what's happening."

She took a deep breath. "Fine."

26

He motioned her to sit beside him at the dining table. "So, let's talk."

"*Great.* We have an audience."

"No, that's just my brother, Merk, plus Levi and Ice," Terk said calmly. "Maybe not even all of them need to stay for this. However, they already know the details, as much as anyone."

"How can anybody *know* them?" she asked, shivering.

"I get it," he stated, his voice firm. "But you have the information in your head, and we need to know as much of it as we can." There was a certainty in his voice that she knew something, and he wouldn't leave her alone until she told him what it was that he wanted to know.

"You do realize," she replied, "that I might not know anything, right? That I might have just been a random person picked up off the street or something?"

"That's possible," Terk admitted, "but I don't really live in a world that is random like that. There is always a pattern and a reason for everything."

She stared at him in shock. "Seriously?"

He nodded. "Seriously."

She grew more nervous by the second. "I don't really think I need that kind of mind-set right now."

"Too bad. We need answers. And that means we need to discuss what's going on."

"There's nothing to discuss," she argued, showing her palms. "I don't know anything."

"Then it won't matter. Now come on. Let's sit down and go over this."

She reached up to touch her forehead, her hand shaking involuntary.

He immediately stopped. "Did you have a ring on your

finger?"

She looked down at her fingers, frowning hard. "What are you talking about?"

"There's a faded mark."

"Yes," she replied. "It is a faded mark and a faded marriage too. That happens sometimes."

"Did it end peaceably?"

"It was right after school and lasted less than a year. So does any divorce end peaceably?" she asked him.

But there was absolutely no give in his voice ... or in the look on his face.

"Fine, so it didn't end peaceably. It was ugly and brutal. I do my best to forget about it."

"Was having children part of it?"

She stared at him in shock, and an ugly sinking feeling in her stomach set in. "Yes, I wanted a family, and he didn't."

"Did you do anything about it?"

She nodded slowly. "Yes, I went to a fertility specialist, but that was a very long time ago."

"Did you ever freeze your eggs?"

At that, she stared at him. She had a feeling this was going somewhere, and she finally settled with the idea that he was damn serious about this and that they needed to get to the bottom of it. She walked back to the dining room, shaking her head. "No, I never froze eggs. At least, I didn't *knowingly* freeze any eggs."

"Good, because there is a difference."

"Not so much in my world," she said bitterly. "In my world people are nice."

"In your world people *were* nice," he corrected, "but your world has butted up against mine."

She stopped and stared at him. "Are you saying that all of this has been done to get back at you?"

"I believe so, yes."

She sat down hard at the dining room table. Ice was still here, as was Levi. She blindly stared at the both of them. "What did I ever do that would make someone think they could use me as a pawn?"

"I don't think you did anything," Terk replied, "but, for one reason or another, you were perfect for their needs."

She stared at him and swallowed hard. "Jesus, would sure help if I could remember something,"

"Maybe we need to do something to shake that loose."

"Shake what loose?" she asked, staring at him.

"Your memories," Terk replied.

Ice frowned at that.

"There are some noninvasive methods, no drugs involved," he immediately told Ice. "Even hypnosis could probably give us a solid lead."

"I don't like the idea of anything happening to me while I'm not aware," Celia cried out. "It's already bad enough to think that I ended up in this condition somehow, and I don't know anything about it."

"Of course," Terk agreed, with that same unflappable spirit, "that's perfectly understandable." After pausing for a moment, he continued. "Would you trust Ice to watch over you?"

Celia nodded. "More than anyone else, yes. Maybe with a recording done that I can hear afterward? Still ... *afterward* worries me."

"Yet don't you want answers?" Terk asked.

"Of course I want answers." She stared at him. "I really do."

"Then here's the deal," Terk said. "We need to trust each other and to do whatever we need to do to get some answers."

THE MEN STEPPED out of the room to have a more private conversation. Terk wanted to do the hypnosis himself, but he was getting flak from both Levi and his brother.

"It'll be much harder for her to relax around you," Merk declared, his voice very stern. "You need to understand that. She already feels like she has been taken advantage of in the most intimate way, and interrogation is making her vulnerable."

Terk stared at his brother, hating the logic of his answers. "Then you do it."

Merk looked at him and then shrugged. He had been gearing up for more argument and was glad that Terk could see his point. "I can do that, no problem, but you'll need to follow my lead."

"That's fine, as long as it's one of us," Terk replied. "I don't trust anyone else with it, and the last thing we need is other people brought in."

At that, Levi nodded. "I don't disagree, which is why we hadn't pursued that avenue already. We've got enough uncertainty and questions without complicating things further." He looked over at Merk. "Are you comfortable with doing that?"

Merk nodded. "Yep, as long as she's okay with it."

When they approached her, she frowned and looked over at Ice.

"Stay calm," Ice stated. "We'll all be here with you."

That reassurance seemed to aggravate her even more. She turned, then snapped, "What? *All* of you?" she asked bitterly. "Like I'm some kind of a show?"

"Who do you want with you then?" Terk asked.

"Not you."

"Too bad," he replied immediately. "I'm the one who has to be there in order to sort through the questions and answers, looking for connections. We need to see where this is going."

She took a deep breath. "I want Ice with me then, as my advocate."

"You know you're not in trouble with us, right?" Merk asked.

"Doesn't matter if I'm in trouble or not. I've already been taken advantage of once. I don't want it to happen again."

"That's fine," Ice agreed. "I'll be with you for sure, every step of the way."

Celia looked over at Terk. "Are you sure you need to be there?"

He frowned. "I don't have to necessarily be right there in the same room, but I do need to give Merk the questions and interact with him."

"Well, if you have to do all that, then you might as well be there. Let's just get it over with."

He gave her a ghost of a smile and shrugged. "I agree. We need to do this soon." He looked over at Levi. "You ready?"

"Yep, I sure am. What's the deal with your team anyway?"

"I don't know. I suspect they're on the way here." Terk paused. After a moment he added, "Even though I told them otherwise."

"I don't think everybody's coming," Ice stated, looking at him. "Damon and Calum are, at least."

Terk nodded. Despite the fear that they would be in danger again, it was nice to know that they cared enough to come and lend a hand. He looked over at Levi, "Do you have room for them?"

He snorted. "We have loads of room here. We could potentially house the entire team."

"Well, don't say that." Terk laughed. "I wouldn't put it past them all to ignore my directions and to show up. They hate missing anything."

Levi laughed too. "Wouldn't surprise me in the least. You have a good team for good reason."

"It presented quite the problem, as they came out of their comas, one by one," Terk shared. "Barely able to move, they each woke up, ready to fight and pissed off because they'd missed out on the earlier action."

"That's funny, but I'm not surprised. They're good men, and, when something happens to one of them, you know it happens to all of them."

"I was trying to keep them all safe and shielded, while they couldn't protect themselves." Terk groaned, sounding a little choked up.

"It's amazing you were even able to do that," Ice murmured. "We could have lost you then, if you'd gone too far, you know? Now they're just trying to make sure you're okay."

"I know." With a shake of his head, he took a deep cleansing breath and turned his gaze to Celia.

She stared at him with a haunted look.

"Look. If you don't want me in the same room, it's fine.

I understand. Maybe Merk and I can talk through headsets," he suggested, "but I'd like to see your facial expressions, your body language. There's a chance we'll have to do it again, if I can't get the questions the first time."

At that, her shoulders sank. "Fine, we can just do it with you there, but I want it taped."

He looked at her and then nodded like he understood perfectly. "That's fine. Then you can see the recording afterward, if you like."

She hesitated, and he needed to get it out there, "Look, Celia. You've trusted Levi and Ice this far. Just keep trusting a little bit longer."

"Easy for you to say."

"No, it isn't. It's not easy at all. I know what miserable shits people can be. Everybody in this room has been through a lot and has seen the results of what horrid people will do to another human being," he explained, his voice soft. "Trying to protect the innocent, always working within the parameters of reasonable and acceptable behavior, well, that's not easy either." Then he looked at Celia, with a small smile. "So, how about we go forward on trust and get through this as quickly as we can?"

She nodded, then looked over to Ice and asked, "What do I need to do?"

"Just sit comfortably where you are, or you can lie down, if you prefer. Just get comfortable, that's the main thing," she explained gently. "We'll get you some food and a cup of tea afterward."

She held up her hands. "I'm already shaking."

"Exactly. That's why we'll do this first and get it over with."

With that, they sat down together. Levi took off to go

check on security parameters. They needed to stay ahead of any problems and make sure that everything was okay.

"Where is Stone?" Terk asked, looking up suddenly.

"He's at the computers," Ice replied, looking at Terk with a questioning expression. "Is there a problem?"

"I'll talk to him afterward."

"Or, if you have a message, just say it." Stone's voice hurtled from the walls. This team had thought of everything in their security system. "Terk, you got a problem, man?"

"Could you take a look on the north side of the property? Something's approaching that way."

"Will do."

With that, Ice shot him a hard look, and he shrugged. "I don't know what the hell it is."

"Let's do this," Ice snapped. "We need to get some answers, before things start to get uglier."

AND, WITH THAT, Merk started the hypnosis process. Slowly and carefully, he calmed Celia down and helped her unwind. He began to ask questions, and she was doing her best, trying to answer, until came a moment where she froze.

"What do you see right now?" he asked softly.

"Men," she cried out. "Two men, two men. ... Oh my God, oh my God. They ... They're grabbing me."

This was important, and he needed to press gently. "What are they doing?"

"They're putting me ... putting a hood over my head." She tried to grab at her face. Then slapped her hand over her upper arm. "Ow."

Immediately Merk brought her back slightly. "Remember now. ... Nobody can hurt you here. You're safe," he whispered. "Those men are already gone. They've already done this to you. You're just trying to figure out what happened. It's just a memory, so keep yourself calm."

She took a little breath and relaxed slightly. "Bastards."

"What do you remember after that?"

She shook her head. "A van. ... Wait. I'm in a van, I'm awake. I'm awake. They're opening up doors and telling me to get out, taking off the hood. I don't even know who they are. I don't know anything about them," she cried out, shivering. "But they're putting me out on the road, and that's when ... first I see crates, full of piles and piles of uncovered wires, in the van. I think that container is full of explosives. Then I see the compound." And the terror once again took over her voice, as she began to panic.

"Celia, remember," Merk repeated, his voice so calm and patient. "This isn't happening now. It's all over with. You can just relax and step back. You are safe."

She took several deep breaths. "Oh God."

"Do you see the men's faces?" Merk asked.

"They have masks on."

"Of course. Is anyone around, is anyone on the road, or anything you can tell me?"

"There's one guy. One, but I can't really get a good look. I can't see his features very much. He won't let me see him, but he's in front of the van."

"Okay," Merk murmured, as he looked over at Terk. "Do you have any idea how long you were there? Think for a moment. How did you feel?"

She shook her head. "My body is sore. And I feel very ... disconnected somehow. Like I'm drugged or something."

"Do you know what they did when they held you?"

She shuddered. "No, and I don't want to know," she cried out in pain. "I was a captive, and I don't know what they did. I don't know why they let me out here. I don't know anything. I'm terrified. They told me to just keep walking up to the next house."

"And then do what?" Merk asked.

"I'm supposed to say hi."

"Say hi?" he repeated. "Do you know what happened?"

"I know when I got there, the gates opened, and I was surrounded," she murmured. "I was still so scared and so shocked."

"Of course you were," Merk agreed gently.

"They took the explosives that were strapped to my body. Someone called out and said I was fine. But I don't feel fine," she remarked. "I don't remember more. It's all a blur. It's like, I just collapsed."

Terk looked over at Ice, who nodded. "Yes, she was basically cognizant and about to walk, but suddenly something they gave her had a delayed reaction and took her out. She literally just dropped." Ice spoke to Celia directly. "It appeared that you reacted to that drug severely, and it took weeks before you surfaced."

Celia nodded. "But I still don't know what happened from the time I was originally kidnapped until the time I was released." Then she opened her eyes and stared around the room. "Jesus, it didn't even work, did it?"

And Terk confirmed she was out of the trance. He smiled at her. "It did work," he corrected her in a quiet, gentle voice. "We got what little information there was. Unfortunately it seems like they just kept you drugged and were proficient at it."

"Of course," she noted bitterly, as she rubbed her hands

together. "I'm supercold," she murmured. She looked over at the three of them. "Can I leave now? I just … I don't want to do this anymore."

"Absolutely," Terk agreed, and he walked over to help her to her feet. "Let's go get you some food." Then he walked her to the kitchen.

Alfred looked up and smiled at seeing the two of them together. "Now that's a sight for sore eyes," he murmured.

"Might be the only sight for a while," Terk replied, then nudged her gently toward Alfred. "She needs something to eat. Plus she's cold and shaky."

"I've got a nice cup of hot tea for her. I made one for her earlier, but she left it. So this is a fresh cup."

Terk sat her down at the kitchen table. "How about food? She looks a little disoriented."

"Yes, maybe some food," she suggested, then looked devastated when he backed away. "Where are you going?"

"I'm not sure what's approaching the house," Terk replied. "You just need to rest now."

"Was anything I said helpful?"

"It helped in some ways. Maybe not so much right now, but we'll figure it out."

She frowned at him.

He chuckled. "You gave me what you knew, but they didn't let you in on anything. And you did see one man's face but not enough to really identify him, according to what you said."

She nodded slowly. "I am a little bit hazy."

"I'll give you some images to take a look at, and Ice will show you the video."

She frowned. "It won't make any difference. Like you said, I could barely see them."

"That may be true, but we'll just try anyway," Terk added. "It's a simple-enough job. You just need to relax, sit in front of a screen, and take a look. That's all."

She nodded. "Okay, if it will help." He patted her shoulder and walked away, when she called out, "Wait."

He turned and looked at her.

"I just understood. Like really understood something. You are just as much of a victim in this as I am. For that, I'm sorry."

He looked at her, then reached out to take her hand. "Me too, Celia, for all three of us." And, with that, he headed out. His heart was heavy, and, despite everything, he felt overwhelmed. After everything he'd seen and heard, this was the most devious, disconcerting, and violating experience he could recall. The complete disregard of innocent life was getting to him.

To think that the child in her womb, with absolutely nothing to do with his fight, would be used as a pawn by someone? Knowing it was his son ... that this was all planned so long ago? It all shook him to his core.

It was his own child.

A child he never expected.

A child conceived without his knowledge.

A child being carried by an innocent woman who had been pumped with drugs. He had to wonder what the drugs had done to the developing fetus.

He could never have imagined having a child added to his life in this way.

The mother of his child was distraught, and, as she'd finally come to the realization and could refer to him also as a victim, he felt even worse. It blew him away that all of this was happening while he'd been in the process of shutting

down a government operation that took everything from
him.

Somehow Celia had fallen into the parameters of what
these guys were after and apparently was on the spot for
whatever they had decided the end game was. Or maybe it
was a backup plan. Terk didn't know.

But somehow somebody she knew was a part of this.

He couldn't imagine that she was just randomly picked
off the street.

She had to fit some criteria.

He wondered about her ex-husband, but she didn't want
to talk about him. As he walked into Stone's control room,
Stone looked up at him and greeted him. "Hey, man. Good
to see you."

Terk smiled, then nodded. "You too." He smacked him
on the shoulder. "What a shitstorm."

At that, Stone chuckled. "I always thought our lives over
here were always more or less a shitstorm, but then I look at
you. This is a whole new level, and I really hope this calms
down soon."

"I don't know how the hell to calm this one down," he
said, while staring at the security cameras. "That woman has
been to hell and back."

"She has, and, now that you're here, maybe you can
make sure it doesn't continue."

"Yeah, I really hope so, but, at the same time, she's carrying my child, and neither of us know how it was
conceived. That is the equivalent of landing in the middle of
the tsunami without a lifeboat."

"I know that everybody is probably asking you the same
thing."

Terk looked at him expectantly. "About what?"

"About the child. What possible reason could anybody have to knock her up with your child?"

"I only wish to hell I knew."

"I was wondering about that." Stone added, "Did you ever think it's because of your abilities?"

Terk froze. "What do you mean?"

"Did you ever think that maybe somebody is attempting to recreate your abilities by using your own sperm? A biological clone of a sort."

Holy mother-fucking hell.

CHAPTER 3

C ELIA WASN'T SURE what to think of Terk anymore. After she heard Levi and Ice talking casually after Celia's hypnosis session, about Terk's abilities, Celia cornered Ice in the dining room the very next morning. "I heard a rumor."

"Yeah? What's that?"

"That all of this is some elaborate scheme to reproduce Terk's abilities. That someone somehow went to all these lengths, hoping for those talents to be passed on to this child."

Ice sighed. "That is a theory, one of many," she confirmed. "We're not sure, of course, but it's a good one, as theories go. But we're not certain how any of this works," she noted calmly. "The bottom line is, we don't have any answers, and everything is on the table, as we do what we can to try and sort it out."

"Well, somebody needs to tell me what Terk's ability is, so I understand why somebody might think that he would pass it down to a child."

Again Ice hesitated.

Celia searched the woman's face. Celia was hoping they were friends, but something was definitely going on here. "I get that people are hiding something from me, and it's making me very nervous. I feel like I've dealt with enough

41

secrets already."

"And you have," Ice agreed, with a nod. "This is just … personal, and the information you seek is not mine to share, and, well, it stretches some people's beliefs."

"In what way?"

"Psychic and some metaphysical abilities maybe."

"If you don't want to tell me, that's fine," she snapped, certain she'd just been given a load of BS, but, as soon as Celia looked at Ice, such surety in her expression that it changed everything. Some truth was here, and now her own instincts were quivering. Celia sat back. "What does that mean?"

"Terk can tell you better."

"Interesting."

"Why?" Ice asked.

"Because … No. That was too far-fetched for this."

"Celia, if you have something to share, this would be a really good time to do it."

At the same time, Terk walked into the kitchen and poured himself a cup of coffee, then headed to the window. Distracted, he didn't even see them.

Celia bit her lip, not willing to share when nobody else was.

Ice nudged her gently. "The only way we'll get to the bottom of this is if everybody opens up."

"You mean, like why somebody won't tell me what Terk's ability is?" she muttered out loud, staring directly at Terk.

Hearing her voice, Terk was roused from his musings. "Sorry, what was that?"

"I want to know what is so special about you? Why you?"

His gaze suddenly narrowed, and he gave a clipped nod. "I guess that's fair." He sat down beside her.

With Ice on one side and him on the other, Celia suddenly felt squished between two very large personalities. Yet oddly enough, she didn't feel threatened. It was a strange feeling, almost as if she were protected. She frowned and tried hard to refocus her attention on what Terk was saying.

"I know things," Terk claimed, with a shrug. "I don't always know what I need to know, and I certainly don't always know things that would be helpful," he explained, "but I get premonitions, and ... I work with energy. I assembled a team with varying abilities of their own, and we've been quite effective as a unit."

"Doing what?" Celia asked.

"We were a black ops division of the US government stationed out of Paris," he explained. "Just after they shut us down out of the blue"—he stopped to collect his thoughts—"my entire team was attacked."

She sucked in a breath and stared at him, wide-eyed.

"I haven't ruled out our own government's involvement. Subsequent attacks have continued."

She winced at that. "Why would anyone do that?"

"Because we know too much," he stated boldly.

Such honesty was in his voice that she didn't doubt him. "Know too much or can do too much?"

His lips twitched at that. "If it was the government, I can only assume it's because they decided we were dangerous."

She sucked in her breath, and he looked over at her, with a gaze so intense, it sent shivers down her spine. "Dangerous in what way?"

"We can do things," he said, pinning her with a sharp

look that she felt to her soul. "We know things that nobody else should be allowed to know." He shrugged. "But, if you're thinking that I know what you did yesterday or something like that, you're wrong. I can't read your mind either." He shook his head. "I get hit out of the blue with all kinds of stuff, sometimes helpful, sometimes not."

At that, Merk walked into the room, sat down, and looked at them sitting side by side. "And Terk can do a lot more than that, which is why he was recruited by the government in the first place. And, since he's been there, they have successfully completed an amazing number of missions. But sometimes the creation becomes something beyond the original intent, and not all have the ability to contain it or to control it."

Celia sat back and felt everything inside her stilling, given this information. "I might have an idea," she murmured, "about why I was chosen."

Immediately everybody turned to look at her, and she looked over at Ice and nodded. "I was right."

Ice reached across to pick up her chilled fingers, then gently squeezed her hand. "Go on."

Celia took a deep breath, but just then Levi walked in. Realizing that something important was going on, he sat down. She took a deep breath. "I ran a test group, doing research on psychic phenomena," she admitted. "I'm a scientist, and I was researching superhuman abilities and the possibility of the impossible. I had grants for studying all kinds of abilities," she murmured.

Terk looked at her. "Like the *electrodes to the head* testing?"

She smirked. "Well, I suppose that's one way to test, but that's not the way I was testing. We were doing a lot of work, especially with aquakinesis, what some might think of as spoon-bending stuff."

Terk nodded slowly. "And what makes you think that would have put you onto somebody's radar?"

She looked over at Terk and saw the understanding in his gaze. "My research would do that. Particularly if Stone's theory is right."

"The one about creating more of you?" Merk asked, an eyebrow up.

"Yes." Terk looked over at Celia. "You were doing the testing because you have abilities, don't you?"

She nodded slowly. "I do, but it's not something that has ever really been ratified. And honestly, they've been very dulled since I woke up here. From the drugs I suppose, so I am not sure I have any now."

"Ratification is for governments," Terk noted. "For those of us in the field, it's not something we need."

"Might not be something you need," she murmured, "but competing for grant money to study it means you have to have some proof. Now"—she shrugged—"I might need a career change."

"How well-known are you in your field?"

She shrugged again. "Not at all really, but there was definitely some outcry when I got the grant money. A few detractors thought I had abilities to somehow influence the grant award decision."

He snorted at that. "Not sure what abilities you have." He studied her with that same liquid gaze that rattled her spine and seemed to see right through her.

Celia stated, "I can sense energy." She wasn't sure if that would be enough for them. She didn't want to go into too much detail at this point.

"Nice."

He was trying to put her at ease and obviously saw what she wasn't saying.

"Give them time to resurface. Drugs can blunt them for quite a while."

"So someone decided that a cross between the two of us would make children who would do what we do?" Celia asked Terk.

"I have no idea," Terk murmured. "Of all the crazy things I've dreamed up over time, that is not one that occurred to me."

She snorted. "Well, I'm not the kind of person who walks around expecting terrorist groups to be looking for a secret weapon either."

"No? That's my department," he said, with half a smile. "But somehow taking my sperm and utilizing it in this way never occurred to me."

"Is that even possible?" Levi asked, his tone somber.

Ice immediately nodded. "Yes, sperm can be aspirated many ways, but I keep going back to the fact that you'd have to be unconscious."

Terk's gaze lifted, and he studied her for a moment. "I was in the hospital, remember?"

"I do, and, from what you told me, you were comatose for a few days."

"A little longer than they thought was normal," he murmured.

At that, she winced. "What are the chances you were deliberately put under? Deliberately attacked for just this reason?"

"Probably way too high for my liking," he replied. He crossed his arms, then leaned back against the chair, but it was obvious from the ticking of a muscle at his jawline that the news bothered him.

At that, Ice turned and looked at Celia. "What about you?"

"I was supposed to have an ovary removed because I'd been having some problems."

"Was it about the same time?"

She winced. "Yeah, you could say that. Also at the time I was having trouble with a stalker. And honestly, I didn't have any remembrance of it, but I assumed that I'd been attacked and raped by him."

At that, Terk sucked his breath back. "Well, you can bet it wasn't me."

She looked at him. "And you can bet I had nothing to do with what happened to you. And yet, the bottom line is, this child exists."

He looked at her and repeated, "*Child?*"

At that, her lips twitched. "I know. I was trying not to say it out loud."

"Say what?" Levi asked, confused.

"What's going on?" Ice asked, having picked up on interchange between them.

"I'm carrying …" Celia began.

At the same time, Celia and Terk voiced the ultimate truth together in unison.

"Twins."

THE ROOM ERUPTED in laughs and congratulations.

Terk sensed the power coming off her like he hadn't in all the time that he'd been here. And that meant she had some way to make it look like she either had no power or, for whatever reason, had been conserving it. "Were you hiding your gift?"

She made absolutely no mistake about his question. She slowly nodded. "I find it easier. Particularly as I recover."

"Of course it is," he agreed, with a nod.

"Hiding what?" Ice asked. "Twins? That's awesome."

"Her power," Terk murmured. "She's been keeping it hidden, so she didn't have to answer unnecessary questions."

"And to keep it safer," she added matter-of-factly. "It's been hard to know what's been going on. Self-preservation took over."

"Has that been a problem for you?"

"I don't know many people like me," she replied, studying him carefully. "Some people with abilities aren't the most comfortable to be around."

He gave her a ghost of a smile. "That's true."

"So wait. Let me get this straight," Levi said. "Somebody knew about Terk's abilities, like maybe a foreign power. It's possible they also knew about you, perhaps because of the accusations regarding the grant?" He shook his head. "But it still seems like a huge leap for them to then decide that the two of you should have children. And because it wasn't likely to happen naturally, they went through all that to create this pregnancy? But why wouldn't they just take the fertilized egg and put it in a surrogate? Why go through the rest of this?"

Terk looked at him and in a flat voice, asked, "How do you know they didn't?"

Celia sucked back her breath at that. He turned to look at her and nodded. "We have to consider that, if they did this once, there's a good chance they did it more than once."

"With our sperm and egg?" she asked in a faint voice.

"I don't know, but it's a valid question."

"Yes," she agreed softly. "Maybe they thought that we would …" She hesitated, as he waited. "I don't know, maybe open up their abilities by raising them."

"That is a possibility," Terk noted, "and obviously you were better for that than me."

She snorted. "While I'm carrying it anyway."

"*Them*," he reminded her.

She winced, "Them, I know. I keep trying to avoid that thought."

"Why?" Ice asked, fascinated.

"It's just feels like such an overwhelming responsibility as it is, but two?" Celia shook her head. "I don't even know what to think about that. Especially not knowing how I got this way. I'm afraid of how I'll react to them, how I'll treat them."

"Understood," Ice agreed, studying her features carefully. "But it'll help as we find more answers. Plus, you've already connected to them in a healthy way, it seems."

"Hopefully, yes," Celia noted. "And the issues seem to be growing as we learn more, which seems backward. The question now is whether or not it's really my egg and Terk's sperm. Also, has it happened again and are there other embryos out there somewhere? That's the hardest part, now that he's verbalized it." After a moment, she looked at Terk, her brows furrowed. "Presumably, if you *know* things," she said, with emphasis, "would you know if there are others?"

"Potentially yes," he replied. "However, just because there might be others, that doesn't mean that they are viable or that they aren't in cryogenics or sitting somewhere dying in a Petri dish."

"I get that," Celia said, "and I really hate to even contemplate that it might be better for them to be in that state, but I surely don't want them raised by anybody else."

"Agreed," he murmured. That left a ton of things for them to sort out, but he agreed with her, at least in part. He didn't know anything about her, except the idea that she was a scientist dealing with this kind of work was fascinating. He'd never met anybody who studied this phenomenon.

That brought up a million questions, but he held them back because they were hardly pertinent to the conversation of the moment. "That does seem to resolve the issue of why you were chosen."

"Maybe," she murmured. "At least it gives credence to the one theory. But it could have been something completely different. It could have been completely random."

He stared at her. "In your line of work, does coincidence come up much?"

She took a deep breath. "No." She shook her head. "Never."

"Exactly," he murmured. "So, I highly doubt that it was a coincidence or a random act. Back to when this medical session happened for you," he asked. "Were you in Paris?"

"England," she murmured. "And you?" She already knew the answer, but this was important.

"I was in England too, and it would have been a fairly short scenario, and then I was back on my feet again, supposedly having healed very well."

"So," Merk noted, "the accident potentially could have been staged and your injury could have just been a total sham. That's only one sensible presumption."

Terk nodded slowly. "If any of this makes sense, and somebody is trying to raise an army," he murmured, "this is a hell of a way to go about it."

"If that's the case, why release me then?" The bewilderment in her voice made him send a gentle stroke of energy across her shoulders. A little reassurance that she wasn't alone.

"Because it's a well-known fact that all children do better with their parents, and all expectant mothers do better if they're not in captivity. So, from the kidnappers' perspective, as long as they kept track of you, they could come after you and the child at any time. Or even at such a time it was proven that their experiment was successful."

"So, release me only to steal my children later?" She gasped in horror.

"Well, that's one theory," Terk clarified, with a nod, hating to contemplate such a plan himself.

Merk added, "It's also possible that they were waiting to see if the twins had any abilities, since, of course, it's certainly not guaranteed." Merk motioned at himself. "I don't have the same abilities as Terk."

"No," Terk said, "but it's not that I necessarily have abilities that you don't, but mine are more defined, whereas it hasn't been your focus."

Merk nodded. "Still isn't. I find that stuff kind of freaky actually."

Terk snorted. "Of course it's freaky. But, in my case, I could never shut it off, so I learned to control it." He looked over at her with raised eyebrows, as she nodded immediately.

"Yes," she shared, "it started when I was about four. My deceased grandmother came to me and told me that I would have to look after me and my mother, so I think Grandmother had some of the genes too."

"Not exactly what a four-year-old wants to hear," Ice noted.

"And hardly appropriate," Terk said, fascinated.

"No, but my grandmother knew that my mother was an alcoholic and was not likely to spend her time looking after me."

"Sorry to hear that."

Celia shrugged. "I know perfectly well what it's like when you're raised by somebody who shouldn't have been a parent in the first place. The fact is, I stayed out of foster care as long as I did by keeping my mother relatively functional," she added. "But it was not easy, and I don't think I did a very good job of it."

"It was hardly your job to do," Terk protested.

"And yet it's the guilt that always stays with you, isn't it?" she asked, looking at him directly.

"Guilt is always something that's hard to get rid of," Levi confirmed. "Any chance your mother had the same abilities, and that's why she drank?"

"That's what I suspected, yes, after she died," Celia shared. "I know when I told her that I had just talked to Grandma, my mother screamed that was impossible and to never mention it again. Didn't take long to realize that she was scared of that truth."

"Of course," Ice agreed calmly. "There will always be those who can't handle the unknown thrown at them, and those who can." She turned and looked at the Terk. "Any proof that our government would have done this?"

"You know as well as I do that there's a good chance they would have, yes. Would they have gone as far as kidnapping Celia and aspirating sperm from me while I was unconscious? Well, that certainly would have taken a lot of planning, which is not beyond them either. But, ... no, I would hesitate to say this pregnancy was due to them directly."

"Honestly, I would suspect that they hired it out," Ice said.

"*Great*," Levi muttered into his coffee. "I can just see the contract advertisement. *Needed, team to steal sperm and eggs for some psychic gestational experimentation.* God, I can't even imagine thinking about it." Levi looked over at Ice.

She nodded. "I know. I'm just thinking about what if that had been us. Obviously it's not because we don't have those abilities, and that's what these people were after." She frowned. "But just the thought of it being our children, well ..."

"Exactly," Celia agreed, with feeling. "So, don't mind me if I get a little emotional about it at times."

"I would think that you would need to be," Ice replied calmly. "And, if you weren't, it would make me even more worried."

Celia snorted at that. "Jesus, there's enough worry going on around here for all of us." She shook her head. "Best thing would be if we could just figure out who did this and put them out of commission to make sure that our children are safe. Then we'll have to figure out what we'll do about protecting the twins, even after that initial threat is taken out."

"Well, we need to figure it out before that," Terk stated. "But, yes, safety is the first priority."

"Absolutely," Celia confirmed. "Though I'm not sure that your idea of safety and mine are the same."

He looked over at her and nodded. "I'm not sure either, but, as long as you have no intention of running away with my children, I'm sure we can come to some kind of equitable agreement."

She winced. "Yeah, you see? When you're pregnant and alone, it sounds great to have a partner, but then when you find out that your partner, someone you've only just met, who was also badly affected, but now wants to have a say in your world, it's not quite the same issue."

"On the other hand," he added, "I'm safe, strong, capable, and I would never do anything to hurt you or the children."

"Well, there is that," she muttered. "Definitely an odd scenario."

He nodded, then called out to the room. "Hey, Stone, you there?"

"Yeah, Terk, go ahead. What do you need, man?"

"Any chance of getting into my hospital records and finding out what might be on them?"

"I can get into the hospital records, sure," Stone replied, "but I can tell you right now, if that's what happened, everything will be hidden."

"Of course it will be," he muttered. He looked over an Ice. "Ideas?"

"Oh, yeah," Ice declared. "When it comes to the medical realm, believe me. I'll get in there and see what I can find. However, as Stone already mentioned, records can be hidden or wiped out completely."

"And what about me?" Celia looked over at Ice.

"We'll probably need a couple things from you, and, first off, what name would any records be under?" she asked. "We searched for Celia Stoneworth, per the ID that you had on you, but we couldn't find anything, so just assumed it wasn't your real name and waited for Terk to get here."

Celia frowned. "That's not my ID. I guess my kidnappers planted that on me to delay you finding out who I was.

My real first name is Philly, given to me by my mother during one of her drinking binges no doubt, but my grandma nicknamed me Celia. I've been called Celia since forever," she murmured. "Legally I'm Philly Waterball, Dr. Philly Waterball to be exact. And, if that isn't a name to make you cringe, I don't know what is," she said. "Going through school was brutal with that."

"I can imagine," Ice replied. "Did you ever legally change it?"

She shook her head. "No. Everybody just calls me *Dr. Celia* in my world."

"We'll pull all the history. All that's available anyway."

"I don't remember a ton of it." She looked over at Terk. "I ended up with quite a bit of memory loss over my whole life after this single kidnapping event."

"I'm not surprised," he told her sympathetically. "If you have the basic info, I'm sure Ice and Stone and Levi can find the rest."

Levi smiled at her. "Hey, that's what we do. So, not to worry. If it can be found, we will get the rest of this down."

"What were you doing in England?" Terk asked. "Where were you staying? How long were you there? We'll track your movements and mine and see where they intersect, if at all. So we can see what we can come up with from that angle, although that also likely explains why you were released by your kidnappers. Everything'll have been erased anyway. Are there any people you remember from your visits back then?"

She nodded. "A few, but the chances of my seeing them aren't very good. I mean, there is the chance that I might remember who they are as my memory returns, or, if I saw them, I might recognize them, but I can't tell you any details at this point."

CHAPTER 4

C ELIA WENT TO lie down soon after the conversation. She was confused, upset, and struggling hard to remain sane through this whole thing. Back when Celia first found out she was pregnant and had heard from Ice how she'd been found, she'd gone through the full gamut of emotions. From hating the father of her child—assuming that she had been raped—to confusion when she realized that the father of her child had potentially been violated as she had been, only now to find the intense attraction that simmered just below the surface for both of them.

That was something she had deliberately kept herself away from, since most people didn't understand the psychic energy, and it ended up just being a hot mess for her.

Yet this energy was an ingrained part of her soul. Then to find out why everything had potentially happened was just one mind-bender after another, and she found it hard to regain a grip on reality.

She crashed onto her bed, thankful to have it, since she didn't even begin to know how to get her life back again. It did make more sense, now that she understood what was going on and how she'd been targeted, but just the thought that others had been targeted in a similar way, or even potentially carried her own children, was beyond compre-hension.

None of it made sense, yet it made an awful sense at the
same time. Her own heartache prevented her from getting
her mind wrapped around it. So far though, everything was
just a shade of dark. Closing her eyes, she soon plunged into
a stupor.

She woke a little later, still groggy. When a gentle knock
came on her door, she called out instantly, "Come in."

She was expecting Ice or one of the other women, al-
though most had left due to the threat of imminent attack.
When she looked up, Terk poked his head through the door.
"Hey," she said, "I guess we do need to talk."

"We do," he agreed. "And the first thing I want you to
know is that I'm not the boogeyman that you've rightly
made out the father of your children to be."

"No, you're right. Sorry that it took so long."

"And just as you know a lot of things in your life, I also
know that the children you're carrying are mine."

"I get that," she replied, "but it doesn't help because I
don't know you."

"No, you don't, but you do know Ice and Levi. Lots of
people can wield energy, and so do you. So you should see
who I am and where I am coming from."

"I don't know that I can trust what I'm seeing." She finally managed to get that out, sensing that incredibly direct
gaze of his.

"That's a valid point too, but humor me. I just want you
to know that I'm not planning on doing anything to steal the
babies or any other dark scenario that is possibly rearing its
head in your mind."

She stared out at him impassively. "Do I seem like I'm
neurotic?"

"No, you definitely don't. But I came stateside, not exactly sure what was going on either. From my perspective, all I knew was that a strange woman turned up carrying my child. A woman I'd never seen before."

"Right," she admitted, trying to quickly shift again. "I keep trying to remember that, but then I just as easily forget it."

"I understand, and it'll take both of us some time to update our information about each other."

"Not that we have a whole lot of time."

"That's another thing I wanted to talk to you about. Ice told me that you refused to go to town. To a safe house?"

"Yes, that's what they wanted, but I don't want to go."

"Even though it might be safer?"

"And do what? Wait? These people have gone to a lot of trouble to create this situation, so I don't think they'll hurt me at this stage."

"It is a big risk you are taking," he cautioned her.

"Not necessarily. If they figure out where everybody else has gone, they could easily go after them as well."

"Yes, that I know. Except that I'm the target, and, therefore, anything to do with me is a target as well."

"Do you think I should go into town?" she asked curiously. He hesitated, and she smiled. "See? You don't agree with that either."

"No, because I feel like I can protect you better here than anywhere else."

She winced. "Well, I would definitely like some assistance in keeping our kids alive."

"That goes without saying."

"Do you have any other children?"

He shook his head. "No, I've deliberately avoided getting into a scenario like that."

She smiled. "Now, when you don't have any choice, look where you're at."

"Oh, believe me," he said, with the ghost of a smile. "I have considered that."

"Meaning?"

"Meaning that sometimes fate takes a hand and puts us in situations that we would never have put ourselves in any other way."

"Well, I can't say I appreciate it myself."

"Do you have any other children?" he asked.

She shook her head. "No, I never seemed to have the right set of circumstances, you know? The time, the lifestyle, the partner who wanted kids. It just never lined up in a way that it seemed like the right thing to do."

"Pregnancy often happens regardless."

She nodded in agreement. "So, you're okay with me staying then?"

"Yes, but there will be a few rules."

"There are always rules here," she stated, her gaze narrowing. "So, are these your rules, or are they extra rules from Levi and Ice?"

He smiled. "Their rules are the ones we always follow when we're here."

"Yeah, I get that, but somehow I feel like you'll have a whole lot more."

"Not to make your life difficult but because we now have children involved."

"Ice knew about the pregnancy from the moment I arrived," she replied.

"Yes, but are you comfortable knowing that he's possibly a target too?"

"You said *he*."

He shrugged. "*They* then."

"I get it. We're all at risk, but I'm not sure what you are saying."

"Well, in addition to the rules that Ice has given you, it would help if we could open a channel between us."

She looked up at him, clearly surprised.

"Not everybody communicates telepathically, but it would be easier and more expedient if I could do that with you, so we could always be aware of what's happening."

"I've never communicated with anybody that way, but, if we can, that would be incredibly awesome."

"Well, I can. My team and I function that way most of the time. At least when energy levels aren't an issue."

That was quite a shock to her. "Wow, it sounds like I could learn a lot from you."

He frowned, then a cloud crossed his face. "I'm not up for being tested."

She giggled. "I get that, and, if I hadn't known it before, the expression on your face just now was loud and clear. I'm not looking to test you in any way. I just find it a fascinating ability that I wouldn't mind learning."

"I'm hoping that you can learn and fast, particularly before we end up with visitors."

"You mean, in the next few hours?" she asked bitterly. "I'm not in the best frame of mind to learn a new trick, especially with a ticking clock, while someone is coming for us."

"It'll be better, once it's over," he promised.

"Of course," she snapped, "but that doesn't make it easier now."

Again that same ghost of a smile appeared. "None of this will be easy, but that doesn't mean that it'll necessarily be difficult either."

"I wish I had your confidence. You've seen this kind of action before, but I haven't."

"That's another reason I'd like to have a channel open."

"Well, if you've taught your team how to do that, tell me how to do it." He looked at her, and she felt a fluttering tendril of energy coming toward her. She frowned. "Is that you?"

He nodded. "Yes, it is. And, if you can feel that, it's a very good sign."

"I feel like it was a test."

He laughed. "It was a probe, just to see if you could pick up on the energy. The fact that you can is excellent."

"I'm not so sure about that," she murmured. "I'm not used to dealing with this stuff."

"I don't know how many different people with abilities you have worked with, but are you sure none of them could do this?"

"Definitely," she stated. "One guy was really good at doing all kinds of stuff that I'd never seen before. Obviously bending spoons is more like a party trick, but he could move items and was fairly adept with it."

"Like?"

"Like locks for one. I lost my keys for the classroom one day, and he just popped it open."

"That would be an interesting thing to learn to do too."

"Is that something you can do?"

"I can do something similar, not necessarily that though. Was he a stable personality?"

"Right. … That's the other part that's always unnerving about dealing with people like this," she noted, "because so many of them aren't stable."

He nodded. "Which is why I'm asking, and why I may not have been the most open when we first met," he explained. "I felt the energy from you, but it was off—muted. I just didn't know what form it would take."

"That's fair. I have certainly met my share of people who were anything but stable."

He smiled. "I'm stable."

"While you are, yet you also aren't. I can see that you've been draining your energy, and, for whatever reason, you haven't recharged as much as you should have."

"I'm still protecting my team," he admitted. "So I've siphoned off a tremendous amount of it to go back there."

"I think right now"—she stared at him in astonishment—"would be a good time for you to let your team sink or swim on their own energy, while you focus on doing what you need to do here."

He laughed out loud at that. "I often wondered if I'd ever make a good father, but, after working with my team, I realized that, if anything, I would be an overprotective father."

She smiled. "Meaning that you're not sure you can let your team go on their own?"

He nodded and shrugged. "Just worried that something will happen to them."

"That's because you've been keeping them alive or keeping them sane for longer than you should have, right? But burning through that much energy is crazy."

He gave her a very small smile. "So tell me. How do you feel about your students?"

"Very protective," she admitted. "It's important that I oversee things, particularly early on, when they aren't as confident. So many are unsure of other people's reactions, having faced ridicule, disbelief, even hate-mongering. ... So, you tell your team that you need them to sink or swim and do what they need to do," she suggested, studying him with fascination. "And I'll tell mine."

"When you cut your threads," he replied, "I'll cut my threads."

"That's fair." She sat here in silence, while he waited. Then she smiled and nodded. "Although I'll need some time to adjust. I wasn't thinking there were many, as my memories are still fuzzy, but I can sense them."

"And you have time, at least a few minutes." And, with that, he disappeared.

He was right; so much was going on, they really just had to get at it and be as reasonable and as sensible as they could be.

That said a lot about him and his concern for the pregnancy. She couldn't do anything but agree with him. She still had to adapt to this new image of who the father was and what had been done to her, but she recognized those adjustments were already happening.

Telepathic communication was not something she'd experienced, much less participated in. The concept tantalized her. Just then she felt that same probe waiting for her to reach out and touch it. She closed her eyes and slowly sent out a response.

The reply was immediately accepted, almost like a computer signal. And then, in a surprise move that she really didn't understand, it felt like she had opened a door.

She gasped, but it was already done, and the doorway waited for her to walk through. She hesitated. What the hell was she supposed to do with that? And here was the biggest part. She was up against somebody who already had a lot of working knowledge and experience, whereas she had just been working to find people like herself. So he was the teacher now, she the student. What a flip.

Now she'd apparently found people like her in a big way. And evidently he had a whole team. The thought just jolted the scientist in her, and she was all excitement and trepidation.

Let it happen. Just let the things take their course.

That was the rational response, but the excitement was bigger than that. The scientist inside her was yelling for joy at having met somebody like herself. And she would have to watch that because she understood instinctively that Terk had absolutely no intention of being studied or tested in any way. He was very much private, confidential. And she understood that because she'd been there.

She wanted into his private world but knew it would take time.

And yet now, still the energy sparked between them.

As she sat at the open door, she heard a voice in her head, almost coming through that open door, challenging her.

Go ahead and walk through it, the voice murmured, *if you dare.*

She glared at that because the last thing she wanted to do was get into a competition, but she was already there. She realized it was pretty hard to not feel exactly the same way he did about all this.

If she could even do that much, it would be huge. She stepped forward a little bit, but she already felt some of the doorway weakening, as if he were closing it because she'd taken too long. She immediately rushed to keep it open, and she felt almost like a tussle of wills commenced immediately.

Then the door closed with a hard *bang*.

She glared at it. "Like hell," she spat. Closing her eyes, she mentally opened up. Almost immediately was a response on the other side, but the door was firmly shut. That frustrated her even more. *Open up. Don't sit there and play games with a door.*

Then she realized that maybe he was keeping her out for a reason. She got up cautiously and looked outside. The lighting was odd, and it took her that long to realize that, while she'd been sitting here thinking about the door, something else had been going on.

She immediately raced to the kitchen. When she got just a little bit closer, she heard an explosion off to the left. It was enough to make the walls around her rattle, even as she reached out to grab hold of anything to steady herself.

What the hell was that?

TERK WATCHED THE explosion from a distance. He turned and looked at Merk with a heavy heart. "You're sure there wasn't any other way?"

"Nope. Once an entrance has been compromised, the protocol is to close it, until we can find a way to safely open it again," he explained calmly. "Don't worry about it. This is my turf."

"I know, but it's also a portent of what's to come."

"Go do your thing," Merk added. "How is it going with Celia?"

"Well, she doesn't trust me, and I get that, but, at the same time, it would be hugely helpful if she did."

Merk laughed. "Not only does she not trust you but

she's still not sure what to even think about you."

"How the hell does that happen when she deals with people like me?"

"She doesn't deal with people like ... *you*."

"No, she deals with people she tests," he noted, with a wince.

"But don't forget, they've also signed up for it."

"Right." Terk shook his head at that. "That is not going to happen."

"Nope, not your thing and maybe not her thing after this because that's probably how she was found."

"I wonder. Imagine thinking that your work is what brought this on."

"I don't think she'd like that," Merk replied, "and why would she? This is way more of a headache than any of us ever thought it would be." Merk faced his brother. "Did you ever do any testing? How else would anybody have known?" Merk asked.

"Hell no. I refused to be a guinea pig. Honestly, I keep coming back to the government," he said. "They were the ones who knew."

"Yeah, me too. I was just hoping someone else was to blame here."

"Well, if you come up with that, let me know, because, at the moment, it's looking very much like it's all about somebody who knew something from within the company. Who else would have known about the work we did?"

"Talk about classified. The US would be the laughingstock if anybody else knew."

"Yet somebody did know."

"Indeed, and that's probably why they were shutting down your team. Which is also an interesting scenario,"

Merk noted, "because, if you think about it, that's not the easiest thing to accomplish either."

"Which is why I was distressed at the time but not panicked about it."

"No, and I'd heard you talk about needing something different in your life."

"I even thought about talking to you about doing something down the road."

"Just the two of us?" Merk asked.

"I don't know. … I'm not sure," he said. "I just felt like change was coming. I didn't really understand where or how and wondered if it was coming from your direction."

"Well, I'm not saying Levi and Ice wouldn't be totally amiable to something," he acknowledged. "There's certainly change here on a daily basis."

"I get that too. And, at some point in time, we have to retire."

"It won't happen," Merk said. "We know where all the bodies are."

"And that's what the problem was," Terk stated, with a gentle smile toward his brother. "Once we know where the bodies are, they really can't let us get away."

"I get it, but, Jesus"—Merk sighed—"did they really have to try to take you all out?"

"I think they thought so. I think they'll regret it though, and maybe they already do."

Merk looked at his brother in alarm.

"No, I'm not doing anything," Terk replied. "I've had more than enough of that. I'm just trying to figure out what to do with the craziness that's happening here, with the upcoming attack."

"Not to mention you'll be a father before long."

"And doesn't that just beat all?" Terk shook his head in disbelief.

"I know that having a family was never part of your plan"—Merk smiled—"but considering ..."

"What? Considering it's already happened? Yeah. Well, ... we will deal with that as we get closer."

"Do you think she'll treat you fairly?"

"I hope so. Neither of us asked for this or could have even imagined something like this happening. So, as long as we keep the communication lines open and keep talking, I'm hopeful."

Merk didn't say anything.

"And you?"

"I'm hopeful for your sake," he murmured. "None of it feels very good though."

"I know, and an awful lot is out there that I don't really understand. I'm just trying to get her to open up a little bit more so we can communicate on a psychic level, but I'm not sure I'm seeing that kind of ability."

"The fact that you can even do that still blows me away," he murmured.

"You could do it too, if you wanted to," Terk reminded his brother cheerfully.

"Yeah, I don't know about that," Merk replied. "I'm very much the pragmatist."

"No way we can be twins without you having the abilities like I do," Terk stated.

"But, like you said, yours are developed. Mine aren't, and I've never been interested."

"What about now?" He looked over at his brother.

"No, not really."

Just then, one of the alarms went off. They raced toward

the center hall to find Levi standing there, glaring at the screens. "We have an intruder on that bottom four acres. A single vehicle that looks like it's setting up some station."

"They may not know that you own that section," Terk said, moving closer to look at the screen.

"It's part of the property I'm looking to own." Levi glared. "At the moment it's just empty space for their operation."

"So, I wonder if they've made arrangements with your neighbor."

"I doubt it," Levi said. "I just made him an offer last night, and they're still thinking about it."

"Doesn't mean that they didn't do this too."

"I would hope not. My instincts say they didn't have anything to do with this. I'm guessing these guys are there without permission."

"Any chance of finding out?" Terk asked.

"Why?"

"We'll roast them anyway, but it would just be nice to know if they had permission first. Also, you need to know how far something like this has gone."

"I'm on it," Merk said. "We need a team of four."

"I'm going with you," Terk replied.

Merk looked at him and frowned.

"Don't even start with me," Terk barked. "Of everybody here, I have the most at stake. Not only has my entire team been attacked but this bullshit of creating children and keeping them from me is too much."

At that, Levi nodded. "Good point, but go to the armory and suit up. Now that you have twins to think about, you have the responsibility to keep yourself alive."

And, with that, Terk took off on a run, following his

brother to the armory, where he put on a bulletproof vest. Finding it odd fitting, he grumbled about it, fussing with the straps.

"Quit your bitching," Merk snapped. "These are new ones, state-of-the-art, and pretty damn decent. We just got to make sure it's adjusted right."

By the time his brother had it adjusted, it felt better. "This is an interesting design. I've not seen these before. They are new, you say?"

"We can talk about that later. But, yeah, it's one of my own designs."

At that, Terk looked at him.

Merk shrugged. "Hey, it's not as if I sit around here and do nothing all day."

"And here I thought you were out on missions all the time."

"I was, but less than I have been," he said sheepishly. "I'm getting soft in my old age."

"*Huh*, I can't see anybody around here getting soft."

"Well, we don't dare let it happen, but, at the same time, you know what'll happen as we age."

"Maybe so or do we just keep bringing in younger people?"

"That's happening too," he murmured. As he settled in, Merk added, "By the way, you're not the only one who will be a father. Katina told me that she's pregnant. So you were right again."

Terk looked over at his brother, and a smile crossed his face. "Well now, that is great news." He laughed. "Do you remember our grandmother's message way back when?"

"Yep," Merk replied. "It's been on my mind a fair bit lately."

"Yeah, I wonder why?" he asked teasingly.

"She said we would have families at the same time. It's just not quite the way we expected it to be."

At that, Terk stopped and then nodded. "No, it isn't, but, hey, I'm nothing if not adaptable."

At the same time, a signal buzzed, and they headed out through one of the secret entrances.

"It's two miles out, so move your asses," Levi snapped in their earpieces.

"Heading out now," Merk replied, then spoke to Terk. "I'll go high. You go low."

And, with that, the two of them scooched down through the pastures and through the intervening meadows to the point where they could see the vehicle in front of them.

Terk crouched low and tapped his earpiece. "I can see them. They are setting up equipment. Hidden but not hidden."

"Well, I think they're hidden enough for them," his brother responded. "It is a pretty concealed little dale, and nobody here would even know to look for it. It just happens to be that we've already mapped this property and set up alerts."

"Smart," Terk murmured.

"We don't leave anything to chance anymore," he explained, "because you know what happens when you do."

"I do, indeed. Shit happens."

His brother chuckled. "Yeah, that's for sure."

With his brother on comm and Levi on the other end, Levi shared over their earpieces how the neighbor had no knowledge of the trespassers. "The good news is, he's agreed to sell me the property. And we're adding that piece for good measure."

"Good. Time to take out the garbage then," Terk said.

When they inched closer, one man talked on a radio. And whoever he was talking to wasn't all that far away because the radio looked like a walkie-talkie.

"That's pretty low-tech," Terk muttered, "but there could be a reason for that."

"They're probably about to start taking out the high-tech equipment. That would be the priority, since they have no idea what it can do."

"Agreed."

All on the same page, they set up a signal to rain hell on the intruders.

"Jesus, that would cause chaos everywhere, so keep an eye out once the shooting starts."

"Does Levi need to shut down any equipment?"

"No, don't even think about it," Merk said calmly. "We have that covered too."

"I'm glad to hear it." Terk smiled. "I'd hate to think that something so simple would take you guys out."

"Nope. It might make Stone scramble a bit to get everything back up and running, but you can bet *up and running* is where we'd be in no time."

"That's good news," Terk murmured. "I didn't really expect anything less."

"Better not." Merk laughed. "Now, shall we go and have a talk with these guys?"

"Well, if it's like anybody else we've had talks with, they won't do much talking. Odds are these guys don't know anything, and, as soon as it's discovered that they've been compromised, they'll be dead."

"Nice guys you're dealing with," Levi chimed in.

"Tell me about it."

"Why don't we get in there and grab them first?" Merk suggested. "That'll give us a little more chance to make some decisions first and foremost. Once we get back to the compound, we can interrogate them with a little bit of privacy and ask any questions we want."

Terk didn't say anything, but he'd seen it time and time again. Still, maybe it would be different here. This was a different group of local hires in a more controlled environment. So maybe they'd have a better chance of surviving a drone shot to kill.

He'd wait and see.

As they neared the trespassing truck, Levi walked up casually, apparently unarmed, and approached the vehicle. "Hey," he called out. "You know you're on private property, right?"

One of the men came around, frowning at him, and replied, "No, sir, we've an agreement with the owner."

"Well then, that's a sorry state of affairs, considering I'm the owner. This property belongs to me." He glared. "So I'd sure be interested in seeing that agreement of yours."

"Well, shit, … somebody must have made a mistake then," the one guy said in feigned disgust. As he turned, Terk felt the hairs rising on the back of his neck.

Without another thought, the man lifted his weapon and fired, as did his companions, but Levi had already ducked and raced around behind the vehicle. Terk took out one of the weapons with a bullet hitting one guy on his hand, square and clean.

The shot gained him a rampage of fireworks. He just waited for it to die down.

In his ear, Merk chuckled. "Nice shot."

"Yeah, I should have killed him though. I'm pretty

damn tired of this shit."

"I hear you there, brother," he said, "but you need answers."

"I don't think anybody here will have them, but we'll do what we can." Almost immediately more firepower turned their way.

Merk waited for it and then murmured to Terk, "They've got something planned."

"They always do. They're pinned down and can't move, but they'll still need a way to get out of there."

"They do. But I'm not sure anybody'll like it."

At that, one of the guys came out with his hands up. "Hey, look. This is just a misunderstanding."

"Yeah?" Levi replied. "What kind of misunderstanding are we talking about? You're on my property. I have the right to pop you right now, and nobody'll give a shit. If you're lucky, I'll bury you, or maybe I'll just let the coyotes have you."

The guy swallowed hard. "Look. I know it's Texas and all, but honestly we thought we had permission. It's typical that somebody would turn around and put us in this position. People are just dicks."

"Yeah, especially the ones who didn't ask ahead of time," Levi said in a hard tone.

"We meant no harm," he said, immediately changing his tune. "We're just looking for a place to spend a few days."

"What place? Surely you can do without private property. It's called private property for a reason, just so you know, and most people don't carry that kind of firepower," Levi said easily. "So you can pack up and leave right now, or you can leave in a box."

"Whoa, whoa, whoa, no need for that," he cried out.

"We're not trying to be difficult here."

"Well, you're also not trying to be easy to get along with. My property is mine, so get the hell out. Now." And, with that, Levi sent another warning shot toward the trailer.

The guy jumped and screamed, "Jesus, I just wanted to talk."

"You've got nothing to say that I want to hear," Levi snapped. "Now move it."

At that, the guy grumbled and went back in the truck, but almost immediately he came back out again. "Hey, how about making a deal?"

"What?"

"I can pay you to stay here."

"Nope, I don't need your money."

"Everybody needs money," he said in a shaking voice. As he walked out, Terk noticed a movement. He focused until he could see one of the other men trying to sneak out the back window. Before he could act, Merk put a warning shot into the back of the trailer.

Jumping, the spokesman turned and looked around nervously. "Jesus, you're not alone?"

"Do I look like an idiot?" Levi asked, with a slow Texas drawl.

The guy swallowed hard. "Look. I'm not from around here. So, I mean, I'm not trying to be difficult. I just don't really understand the rules."

"Oh, you understand the rules just fine," Levi murmured. "You're just happy to break them, regardless of the obvious."

The guy looked increasingly nervous. "Look. I don't want any trouble."

"Then pack up and leave," Levi said, his voice steady and

calm.

Terk had always admired that about Levi. Terk hadn't done too many missions that involved Levi directly, but plenty of times they had dealt with each other him on a multitude of things, including organizing team members and sending out assistance. Terk knew that, whenever something went wrong, Levi was the guy to have in your corner.

Calm, steady, and always on point.

Terk stopped for a moment. "Did you just hear that?"

"Yeah, I did. Sometimes I hear you, and sometimes I don't."

"Wow, it was her," he murmured.

"You might want to tell her that you got her telepathic message because she thinks *I'm* the oddball one."

Terk laughed.

Just then one of the other men stepped out. "Look. We're not looking for any trouble. We'll pack up and leave."

"Right now," Levi snapped, his voice hard. "And we aren't leaving until you do."

The other guy hesitated, and, realizing this wouldn't get any better, he walked over to align the hitch to the truck parked nearby. He backed it up to hook on to the equipment.

Terk watched the whole scene unfold but didn't like anything about it. "This will go bad real fast," he murmured.

Merk replied, "I hear you. I'm sending a message to Levi right now." Terk heard Merk via their headsets.

Ice also felt uneasy. "Yeah, this one's not cool," she said, her voice hard. "Watch your back, Levi."

Levi was no longer there. Terk and Merk searched for him but found no sign of him where he had been earlier.

One of the men swore. "Where the hell did he go?"

One replied, "You can bet he's watching this. They told us to watch out for these guys, but nobody said they were bloody ghosts."

"Well, they are, and I don't like anything about this."

"Hey, just finish the damn job," said the third man from inside the truck. "Then you can go on your merry way."

The two men looked at each other and quickly tried to pack up the trailer, so they could leave. As soon as it was done, one guy called out, "Hey, we're done. We're packing up right now."

No answer.

He looked back into the trailer. "We're almost done here anyway," he said. "Why do we even need to stop?"

"Because you were told to by the angry owner," the other guy snapped, his voice mean and surly.

"Yeah, but nobody said it would be like this."

"Well, the job is finished," he said, "and I'm glad to be leaving."

"Yeah, no doubt." An odd tone filled his voice.

The kid looked around. "What does that mean?" he asked. "I was here doing the job you wanted me to do."

"Yeah, you were," he murmured. And, with that, a single shot rang out. The kid fell from the back of the trailer onto the ground.

Almost immediately, the truck engine turned on, and all hooked up, it drove away.

Terk lifted his handgun and took out the front tire, while Levi jumped out of the far fence line and took out two other tires. Within a matter of seconds, Merk had his gun pointed at the driver's head. "See now," Merk said, "that's just plain mean. We don't take kindly to people killing off their partners."

The driver swore heavily. "Shit," he said, "we'll be in deep trouble for this now. You have to let us go."

"No, we sure don't," Terk added in a bored voice. "You shouldn't have been on this property as it is."

"They told us that it wouldn't be any big deal," he babbled.

"Well, guess what? It is. Now put up your hands and get down out of there." And the two men slowly raised their hands but remained in the truck.

Levi's gun was now pointed at them too. "Remember," Levi said. "Don't do anything stupid. I have no problem dropping you right now."

The one guy complained, "We didn't do anything to you. It is just a piece of property." But his gaze was ever searching the area and looking for something.

Merk walked closer. "All right, keep your eyes on the wheel in front of you." His buddy was already slipping out of the passenger side, and suddenly made a run for it, heading up the road. At that, the driver hit the gas hard and intentionally swerved, striking the other man hard with the truck and trailer, then continued to the top of the hill.

However, the vehicle came to a halt at the top of the hill, where Ice had cut off the driver. The big truck and the gun she had were absolutely not something to be taken lightly.

Levi was the first to arrive at the driver's side door.

The driver looked at him and swore. "What the hell has she got?"

"Looks like a rocket launcher to me," Levi said, with humor in his voice. "When she gets pissed, you really don't want to cross her."

"Holy crap." Obviously the intimidation was working because the driver quickly exited the vehicle and fell to the ground, his hands over his head.

Levi raced over and quickly disarmed him, then rolled him over and tied him up neatly.

Seeing that situation was nicely in hand, Merk joined Terk, gathered where the second man had fallen. "Really stupid on your part to run."

The guy was barely breathing, clearly with terrible internal injuries from being struck and run over. "We ... didn't do ... anything, and ... I didn't shoot my ... buddy. It ... was him," he gasped.

"Maybe so," Merk said calmly, "but that won't save your ass now."

He looked at him fearfully. "Call ... the cops."

"Well, the cops won't help you either," Terk murmured, as he stepped forward. "We just want to ask a few questions."

The guy swallowed hard, gasping. "I don't ... know anything, right?"

"No, we don't know that at all." He glared. "I mean, we suspect you don't know anything because it was a pretty stupid stunt you just pulled, but, at the same time, I imagine you had a reason for doing that."

The kid nodded. "Me and ... my friend needed ... money. His girlfriend's ... pregnant."

"Well, this wasn't a good way to do it," Merk noted. "Now that kid will grow up without a father."

His breathing grew even shallower. "Sometimes ... decisions look decent, ... then turn to ... shit." And, with that, he closed his eyes, barely breathing.

"He's done for. He won't live another ten minutes, if that." Terk bent down to the dying man.

"The way his whole body was crushed, it's amazing he lived this long."

Terk was quiet for a moment, concentrating. "He's gone. Let's go give Levi a hand."

A few minutes later, they had Levi's prisoner on his feet. "Now walk."

And, with that, he looked at him. "Walk where?"

"You're walking up to the compound," Terk said. "Which is up and around that corner."

"Oh hell. I heard that place is like a fortress."

"Yep, it sure is. But you also stumbled onto the heartland down here, so deal with it."

CHAPTER 5

C ELIA HEARD THE ruckus, as everybody returned to the complex. *Dear God, please let everyone I love return safely.* As she raced downstairs, Alfred immediately caught her hand. "Nope, the prisoner is headed down to the jail."

"Jail?" She stopped in her tracks. "I've been here all this time and had no idea there was a jail."

"Ice insisted on it. She wanted a holding cell to secure prisoners."

"Does she get many?" Celia asked in shock.

Alfred nodded. "Way too many for all of us. However, in your case, you need to sit down, have a nice cup of tea, and relax."

She almost chuckled. "How much tea do you think I can drink?"

"Considering that the babies are getting bigger, as much as you need to." He smiled. "But that's okay if you don't want to. We understand babies around here."

"Sounds like a few are on the way."

"A whole lot of them." He puffed up with paternal joy. "And I'm perfectly happy to have every last one of them. All homes should ring with the cheerful sounds of children."

She chuckled. "Even while there's chaos?"

"Yep, that's the way we like it. Some chaos comes with control." He chuckled. "Now chaos without control? That's bad. Babies? We can control."

She murmured, "Do I get to go see him?"

"See who?" he asked innocently.

She frowned. "You know who."

"Oh, …Terk. … Well, he's probably bringing the prisoner up." Alfred pointed at a screen in front of them.

There, sure enough, Terk marched with his brother toward the house, a man in front of them.

"That's really what he does, isn't it?" She'd never seen him like this.

"Yes, that's what these men do. They make the world a safer place for everyone."

"Until it comes back to bite us in the ass." She placed her hands protectively over her belly.

"Even then," Alfred noted, "he will do everything in his power to keep you and the babies safe."

"And what if it's not within his power?"

"Then you don't know the man." Alfred smirked. "And you need to give him a chance to get to know you too. This is what he does in a big way. It's really important work, and he is amazing."

"I hope you're right. I feel like I've thrown my lot in with him, and I'm scared that I've bet on the wrong horse."

"Not at all," he said, giving her some much-needed reassurance. "And it won't be too long before you know that." And, with that, he smiled and patted her on the shoulder. "Now, go sit down."

She groaned. "There's got to be something I can do at least."

"Yep," Ice said, as she came in.

Ice walked right up on them without Celia noticing, and it unnerved her. She was usually more aware—at least she remembered being that way ... before.

"You can look at these three guys and see if you recognize any of them." Ice held out her phone and slowly flicked through three faces on her screen.

Celia frowned at them. "No, I don't know any of them."

"Good enough."

"Was that who you just brought in?"

"Well, we brought in the remaining live one." She sighed. "He killed off his partners."

"How is it that they have so little regard for life?" Celia cried out, staring at Ice. "How can they just kill somebody they hired themselves."

"Apparently that's what this group is all about." Ice continued. "According to Terk, they've been up against these guys time and time again. They kill off anybody in their group if they even *look* like they might be compromised. We'll have our work cut out for us keeping this one alive."

"You think he'll be killed?" Celia gasped.

"If the pattern fits, quite possibly, yes."

Alfred nodded. "If they don't want him to talk to us, they'll try and kill him."

Alfred sounded so certain that a chill crept into the room with his voice. "Good God," Celia whispered.

"That's why he shot one of them outside. Right in front of us." Ice snorted. "Then he ran down the other one with the truck and its trailer. You don't need to worry about this prisoner. He's secure downstairs."

"I'm fine," she murmured, "but it would be nice if everybody wouldn't be trying to protect me all the time."

At that, Ice laughed. "Well, you might as well get used to that because that's what we do. Protection is everything to us."

"I get that," Celia muttered, "but it's a little distressing when you're the *protected little woman.*"

"No, not at all, particularly in this family. Nothing more precious than the children you are carrying, and right now you need to avoid stress." Ice headed out of the room, then turned back to her. "Particularly for Terk, this is difficult. He intentionally never planned to have a child because of the dangers in our world. But now that they exist and you are here," she said, "this isn't something you'll get him to step back from."

"I wasn't planning on asking him to do that," Celia said, her voice choked up. "It's just taken me a little bit to get my mind wrapped around the fact that decent human beings are on the other side of that."

Ice smiled, walked back, and gave her a hug. "It's been a rough go so far, but you're safe, and you're in good hands. So trust us a little bit. It's a big ask, I know. But I feel like we've given you a lot to trust already, so please trust me."

"I already do, more than I ever thought I could trust anybody. I really do trust you, but the work that you do—"

"Takes a little getting used to, I know. However, our people are the best at what we do. And we are always out there, pushing the limits of what we know to be possible. We definitely have problems when hiring staff." She chuckled. "Some people say that they're really good at something, but, when they come up against our measure, they're not even close."

"I'm sure your standards are pretty damn high," Celia added.

"They have to be," Ice muttered, as she walked back toward the kitchen. "The absolute best."

"What about your kids? Where are they? Both boys,

right? And you just had your second one recently?"

Ice nodded. "They are off visiting Grandpa right now," she said, with a big smile. "And believe me. He's thrilled."

"I can imagine." Celia stood and looked out at the helicopters. "Is that how everybody travels here?" she asked in wonder.

"Nope, not everybody, not all the time. There's a huge expense involved with lifting one of those birds," she noted, "but they're mine, and that's how I prefer to travel myself these days." And, with that, Ice turned and walked away.

Celia stood here, staring in the direction Ice had disappeared, until Alfred came up. She turned and looked at him, then asked, "Are those all Ice's?"

He looked at her, then followed her gaze to the helicopters. "The birds? Absolutely. Several people here fly, but she's the one who started this business with Levi, and she's the pilot. Believe me. You don't ever want to cross her when it comes to skills."

"No, I never would. What's amazing is how being surrounded by this incredibly talented group of people makes me feel like I have absolutely nothing to offer." She raised both palms.

"Yet …?"

"At the moment I'm feeling very much like a baby-making machine, and I'm not sure how I feel about that," she said, disgruntled.

He burst out laughing. "I get it, but you might want to remember that just because it may seem to you that it's not valued, it definitely is."

"I don't know," she muttered, as she stared around the place. "I don't even know what this place is. Like, when I arrived, it was full of people, and now it's a ghost town. I mean, I've certainly seen it full of people but not to the fullest level because, I gather, a lot of the team have been out on missions." She shrugged. "You must have a huge organization."

"It is now," Alfred agreed, "but it didn't start that way. It started with just five of us and after that? Well, … things kept growing."

She smiled. "And still you look after everything?"

"I do, along with Bailey. And generally that's all we need. And we're happy without too many people getting underfoot." He chuckled. "Still, if you want something to do, and only when you want to, you can help in the kitchen. Believe me. I won't say no."

She stepped closer. "Put me to work, please. It's tough enough seeing just how incredible these people are, but to think I have nothing to offer makes me feel sad and dismal."

"You're a scientist," he stated. "Why would you even go down that path?"

"Because it's not like what I study is of any value here." She waved her hand toward the dining room. "Terk has more skills than I've seen in my whole lifetime."

Alfred nodded. "And I think sometimes the lesson in life is that, as soon as you think nothing is out there, somebody bigger and better and more skilled than you ever thought possible always appears."

"Well, that's certainly coming true here." Celia walked into the kitchen, saw several big bags of groceries spread out across the counters. "Oh my goodness. I can't even imagine this much food being consumed."

"That's because we are not making food just for today." He pointed to carrots that needed to be chopped and potatoes that needed peeling. "We also use leftovers to make up to-go packages and sandwiches and such. So believe me. There's never any shortage of things to be done in the kitchen."

She nodded, then picked up a potato peeler. "I'm just happy to be useful."

THE GUYS WERE gathered in the hallway, having a private conversation, yet with a direct line of sight to watch their prisoner. Terk stared at the man sitting behind bars. He was bent over, his head in his hands, quiet.

"One man," Levi said. "Just one."

Beside them, Merk asked, "What were you expecting?"

"I was expecting … none," Levi admitted. "So we'll take one. Have any of the ones you've managed to keep alive then lived beyond your captivity?"

Terk shook his head. "Nope, drones and snipers have taken them out."

"Well, it'll be interesting to see if that happens here. This is the guy who took out the other two, so if anybody's got any information, it'll be him."

"But he won't share." Terk studied the prisoner, his energy flat, tight.

"Doesn't matter if he does or not," Levi said. "We've got everything we need to run him down anyway."

"That could give us more leads," Merk suggested.

"Terk, we're on it," Levi stated. "Don't worry."

"I know you are," Terk said. "I'm just damn tired of all this. And the fact that they were most likely part of a setup and could just as easily have been part of a diversion means that we still can't ease up."

"I was thinking the same thing," Levi muttered. "The diversion is one thing, but they didn't look like they were terribly knowledgeable."

"The other two for sure. Just dumb kids, looking for fast money," Merk said. "And, of course, they were taken out before they could say anything."

"Life is cheap for these guys," Levi noted.

"Not only cheap, I don't think they have any limitation on their resources. They seem to have an unlimited supply of grunts too," Terk murmured. "That's pretty depressing as well."

"Yep, but. as you know, we have a pretty strong team here."

"Of course you do." Terk turned toward Levi. "I never meant to imply anything other than that."

Levi chuckled. "Good, it's not me who would be insulted, as much as your brother."

Terk laughed at that. "I think Merk and I understand each other pretty well." He looked over at his brother. "Or am I wrong?"

"Nope, you're not wrong. I'd say we're good. You want to talk to him now or let him stew?"

Terk frowned. "I'd like to let him stew, not that I think it'll do any good. Everything about him as he sits there has a military bearing to it."

"I was thinking that too," Levi murmured.

"All the more reason to let him sit for a bit, while we figure it out."

"If we can get any answers before we approach him, that would be good." Levi walked closer to the prisoner.

"I suspect it won't make a damn bit of difference though." Terk looked over at Merk. "What about you?"

"I say let him stew," Merk replied with a definitive tone.

At that, the prisoner glanced over at him and smirked.

"Yeah, see? … He doesn't give a shit what we do."

"Yeah, well," Ice added, as she walked briskly toward them, "now that we know who he is, maybe we can get somewhere."

At that, the prisoner looked startled.

And Merk smirked at him. "Remember? This is what we do. So you might think that you'll walk scot-free, but that ain't happening. Even if another team is coming in to try to rescue you, we'll make sure you go down in the fire."

The other guy just stared. "You guys don't have the skill."

"And this whole thing has been an ongoing plan for a long time, hasn't it?" Terk asked.

"A long time," he agreed. "Not that you guys had any idea."

"Well, how many people would?" Terk asked him curiously.

"Think about it. I mean, you don't even have a clue that you're being targeted."

"How many people around the world expect to be targeted?" Terk asked.

"Anybody worth their salt," he sneered. "It was time for you to go."

"Yeah? And who made that decision?"

"Your boss, of course." The prisoner laughed. "But I'm sure you don't believe that."

"It's not that I don't believe it." Terk stared at him. "I'm just not prepared to believe it without some proof."

"Poor you. There is proof, of course, but I don't ever expect you to find it."

"You could help us out here a little bit." Ice gave him a half smile. "I mean, after all, isn't showing how smart you are what you enjoy the most?"

"I've already given you enough to go on." He shook his head. "If you guys were any good, you'd have found the information already."

Ice chuckled. "Well, correct me if I am wrong, but you are now known as Jerome Hartley," she read from her tablet, "high school dropout, kicked out of the military, and currently a wannabe?"

"I'm no wannabe," he said, with a snort. "I didn't do well with the military, that's for sure. I do much better in a private organization."

"Not according to this. Apparently some people got rid of you because you were a little too forward-thinking and decided you should dispose of your bosses a little prematurely."

"Hey, the world is all about change. If you don't change with the world, you get left behind. Just like you guys." And then he started to laugh. "God, I can't wait to see the look on your faces when you realize how much has gone on behind your back. I'm really looking forward to seeing that."

"Well, that's presuming you're still around to see it," Terk said. "Obviously my entire team was targeted, and several of them were taken down, but they got back up."

"That's okay. They will take them all down. That's already in progress."

At that, Terk smiled. "I hope so because I know a lot of people who want a second chance at them." Terk appeared completely unconcerned, even had a note of humor on his face. "You're really expecting to be rescued, aren't you?"

The guy glared at him. "I know my team. Too bad you

don't know yours."

"My team can handle themselves."

"Yeah? Like they did so far?" he asked, with a snort. "You didn't even see the knife in your back, did you?"

"That's different." Terk needed to take him down a notch, so he continued. "And you didn't see yours either, did you?"

The other guy chuckled. "Nice try, but I know my team."

"Of course, so you already took out two guys who would just hold you back, right?"

"Exactly. The minute they decided that it was getting to be dangerous"—he shook his head—"they became a liability. You don't go into something like this without being prepared to lose everything. On the other hand, you can also gain everything."

"What? Money?" Terk laughed. "Can't you figure out how to make a ton of that without killing people?"

"Killing people is the easiest way to do that. Big money, with no responsibility, like those nine-to-five bullshit jobs people sign up for." He walked a little closer to the bars of his cell and asked in a whispered hush, "Who the hell wants that anyway?"

"Maybe nobody wants it," Terk said, eyeing him carefully, "but they don't want to kill either."

"More loss to them." He settled back in the chair again. "I'll just sit here and wait."

"You mean, you'll sit here, and hope that, by some miracle, you're right?" Levi asked, with a hard note. "I'd much rather you kept telling us what the hell's going on."

"Well, the fact that you don't even know"—he stared at Levi—"means you don't even realize that your number is up too."

"In what way?" he asked, studying the man.

"Some people have decided that you know too much, that you asked too much, and that nobody should have that kind of ability. Yes. *Ability*," he repeated.

"As in knowledge?"

"Whatever." He shrugged. "Believe me. You've become extraneous too."

"Just like Terk and his team?" Levi asked.

"The fact that you're all connected was just a given right off the bat."

"Maybe so," Ice said, standing beside him. "But your bank accounts seem pretty empty for somebody who talks as much as you do."

"You don't know anything about my bank accounts," he said, with a laugh. "Nice try though."

"Well, I found the Swiss one too. We're hacking into that one right now." That definitely got her the attention she so very well deserved. "You have nothing on North American soil. You have one out of England, which I passed over to MI6. I mean, I owed them a few favors," she said casually. "We'll get into the Swiss one, and maybe move some funds. We can always use more money to fight evil in this world."

"Not possible." He stared at her. But, for the first time, a note of fear entered his voice.

"Oh, it absolutely is," Terk said, with a fat smile.

Jerome shook his head. "You can think about the numbers all you want, but nobody'll hack it," he sneered.

"Not even with the numbers that you're thinking right now?" Terk asked. "Like 3579246."

At that, the other man's face turned pale. "What the fuck was that?"

But Ice already had written down the pin code. "Thank you, Jerome. Couldn't have done it without you. I'm sure we can put it to good use."

"No fucking way. Did you just ... How the fuck did you find that out?" he roared. "That's why the Swiss are so good at this. They're safe."

"They're safe, until you become a liability yourself," Levi noted calmly. "And, of course, the other guys don't believe in your ability either. Still thinking we're off our game?"

"Of course I do." He gave a wave of his hand. "More scare tactics on your part."

Something was still off about the guy, and Terk couldn't quite place it. He studied everything he could about him, but Jerome was laughing hard now. "Then again, I guess you don't really care whether you live or die," Terk said.

"Of course I do," he said, "if for no other reason than to make sure I take out you assholes for stealing my money."

"We haven't taken it yet," Ice said cheerfully, "but I've got it on my list though."

"That's illegal," he snapped.

At that, Terk looked at him. "Did you seriously just say that?"

He glared at him. "You can't just steal my money."

"I sure as hell can," he snapped. "You're here to kill us."

"Not all of you, but, if you all go, who cares? None of you are worth keeping alive. So, if that's part of the deal, I wouldn't worry about it a bit."

"Well, I would," Terk disagreed. "No loss of life is acceptable."

"Yeah, that's because you're one of those Goody Two-Shoes who care," he mocked. He shifted on his chair, rotating his shoulders, as if they were sore.

"True." Terk hoped that Jerome was damn uncomfortable, but he also knew that, if guys like this had any decent training, they wouldn't break early. He just looked over at Ice and shrugged. "Personally I'd take all his money, wipe out the account, and close it, so that, even if somebody else tried to put money in there, it wouldn't go through."

"Not a bad idea that," she said smoothly. "We're just confiscating stolen goods anyway."

"Not stolen," Jerome barked. "I earned them. And you can bet I'm coming back after you, if you touch it."

"You can threaten me all you want." She smiled. "I don't give in to threats. You may have seen my face when I was holding that fucking launcher, and I was prepared to use it. Bring it on."

"Yeah," he snarled, "I've heard about bitches like you. Don't worry. I'll be back."

"That will just get you killed." She grinned broadly.

Jerome could do absolutely nothing, as they had him as a prisoner. The problem would be if he ever got free. Terk looked over at Levi and Merk, who appeared to be studying Jerome, like some insect.

"You know," Levi murmured, "we should have just opened up a cemetery in the back. Or really, a mass grave would work just fine."

"We still can," Ice said calmly. "You know we did check into it, and there were really no substantive obstacles."

"Well, we made a preliminary inquiry," Levi said, with a smirk.

"Considering that the dumb shits who end up dead here are just assholes we don't give a crap about anyway"—she looked at her prisoner—"I'd just as soon take care of it, and the sooner, the better."

"Depends on if he has anything else to offer us." Levi tilted his head. "However, I don't think he's willing to share anyway."

"He's done not too badly so far." Terk smiled. "I mean, those numbers were pretty helpful."

At that, Ice laughed. "Yeah, has he got anything else like that?" she asked, looking at Terk curiously.

"All kinds of numbers are coming up, but not necessarily anything that's making sense. I can share them with you later."

At that, Jerome looked over at Terk. "What do numbers have to do with anything?" he muttered. "And what the hell are you doing that you can even see those numbers?"

"Good enough," Ice turned and headed toward the door, calling back, "If any more bank account numbers pop up, I'd be very interested in those. Jerome can't use them anyway, as he won't be around for much longer."

"Good point." Terk grinned, as he named two banks.

At that, Jerome gasped. "What the hell?" he asked. "How the hell are you getting that information?"

Ice slipped over and looked at Terk. "Any account numbers?" she asked, her pen at the ready.

He studied the guy for a moment, and seeing the digits was not even intentional on his part. "Yeah." He read them off, as Jerome paled quickly.

"What the fuck?" His voice turned deadly. "You won't live long enough to touch that."

"You know what? You won't get to live at all," she said, "so somebody might as well use the money, and why not us?"

"Those are secret accounts," he roared. "Nobody gets into those accounts. You have to have a security form."

"Good," she noted. "Like bitcoins? I'm sure you've got a bunch of that too." She looked over at Terk.

His eyebrow popped up, and he nodded. "Let me see what I can come up with along that line." Terk smiled.

Jerome glared at him. "Are you psychic or something?"

"Or something." Terk chuckled.

"Is that what the fuck this is all about?"

"Isn't that why you were told to kill us?"

"No, we weren't told anything like that." He stared at him in amazement. "Are you serious? Can you really do that shit?"

Terk shrugged. "It's a piece of cake, man. You're like an open book." He smirked. "Not exactly the open book you probably want to be, but you can do nothing to keep that hidden from me. When I really want to go in after something, I can dig really fast. Are you still not sure we brought our A-game?"

"Leave my money alone," he said, his tone ugly.

"Too late. I already gave her all the details. The only thing I don't know about yet is the bitcoin wallet."

"You won't," the angry man replied. "I worked really hard to keep all that shit hidden, and, if you don't have a password, you can't get the bitcoins."

"Yeah, but, with a password, I can get all of it." Terk smiled. "And I don't think it's all that hard to sort out. Your password, I mean." As the code blazed through Jerome's brain, Terk laughed, got out a pen, and wrote it down. Then he walked over and held it in front of the guy. "What do you think about that?"

Jerome freaked out, screaming bloody murder.

Terk handed the info to Levi. "He won't need this."

"Wow." Levi stared at Terk. "I forgot how deadly you

are."

"Yeah, only to the wrong people though. The good thing is, I do have some morals and ethics." He jerked his thumb over his shoulder. "Unlike this asshole. He was hired to take out this entire compound. While he was thinking about all that, I also caught wind of a couple other things flying out there. A group of ten are gathering and gearing up outside, a few miles away. This little asshole party was just the recon crew and not very good at it, as we witnessed."

Jerome stared at Terk in shock. "You need to be fucking put down," he roared. "Nobody should be allowed to do that. Nobody is safe then."

"You definitely are not," Terk growled. "But I never did anything to hurt you and I never did anything to hurt anybody in this country. I worked *for* the government."

"Yeah, you did," he snarled, "but the government was done working with you. They're the ones who put out the contract on you. They're the ones who started this."

"I'm not surprised," Terk replied softly, feeling his heart sink because such truth was in Jerome's voice that Terk couldn't just ignore it. It was truth according to his energy as well, but that could be what Jerome was told—not necessarily what was real. "But you're still not telling me who your boss is."

"The one who shut you all down. He shut you down and then put out the contract to make sure nobody lived past the next few days. He didn't want anybody to know anything about you. Hell, if I'd realized what the hell you could do, I'd have been volunteering to put a bullet in your head from the first go. Before you could read my mind."

"But you didn't," Levi said calmly, "and now you get to watch it all fail."

"How can it not fail when somebody like him is around?" Jerome stared at Terk, like he was some alien. "You need to be put down, like the dog you are."

"I suppose they want to put me down for a lot of reasons." He shrugged. "And, of course, knowing too much is definitely at the top of that list, but, more than that, they're afraid I'll come back after them for what they did to my team."

"They did say something about that. Wanting to make sure that you were taken out permanently, not just temporarily, because you had this bad habit of rising again."

"Yeah, I sure do." Terk stood here and waited to see if any other information floated free from Jerome. When nothing else came up, Terk looked over at Levi. "Don't let Jerome get loose."

"He's not going anywhere," Levi said. "His guys will try to bust him free, just to make sure he doesn't talk."

And, with that, Levi turned and walked away.

CHAPTER 6

C ELIA LOOKED OVER at Alfred. "How much longer do you think they'll be?"

"As long as they need to be," he said gently. "Best if you don't think about what's going on downstairs."

She nodded slowly. "Don't you ever think about it?"

"I was in the navy with Levi," he shared. "So Levi knows the scoop. They all are well-trained and pretty handy on their own."

"I know, and I'm seeing more and more evidence to suggest that I'm not as nice a person as I thought I was."

He looked at her, frowning.

She shrugged. "I'd like some of these guys to disappear permanently. I didn't think I'd ever be inclined to say that."

"Sometimes these guys do need to disappear permanently," Alfred agreed. "Otherwise nobody is safe."

"That's what I meant, I guess," she murmured. "It just seems that assholes like this keep getting away with all kinds of stuff. And those who follow the law can't seem to do anything fast enough about it."

"Which is sometimes why you have to take the law into your own hands."

She sighed. "Is that ever a blurred line?"

"No, not really, and don't forget. You're in Texas. Protecting family is foremost."

She nodded. "And I get that. I really do. It just seems that, right now, … everything is so confusing."

"It was very confusing, but we're starting to get answers now," Alfred reminded her. "As long as answers are popping up, there will be solutions. The team just needs to get a little bit more in the way of information."

"I hope so."

Just then Terk walked in. He didn't say a word, just headed over to the minibar to grab a bottle of water out of the fridge. He cracked it open and poured back the contents.

She watched him out of the corner of her eye.

When he was done, he turned to look at Alfred. "How long until food?"

"About an hour and a half. Are you all right, or do you need something now?"

"I'm okay." He shifted, flexing his muscles. "I'll need to top up soon."

"Foodwise or energywise?" Celia asked.

He burst out laughing. "Not many people even know to ask me that question." He turned to look at her.

"Well, it's the work I do," she said calmly. "Though I've never seen anybody do it quite like you."

"You haven't seen the half of it yet," he responded, and a dangerous edge consumed his voice, as if what had just happened downstairs wasn't something she wanted to know about.

She didn't want any part of it either, but she couldn't help asking, "Is he still alive?"

Terk looked over at her and gave a clipped nod. "He is so far."

"Is that a good thing or a bad thing?"

He shrugged. "He's given up way more information

than he thought he had, so I'm sure he's cursing us pretty well."

"That's his problem. He shouldn't have crossed us."

"Yeah, and that's what gets us down that pathway," he murmured, as he studied her carefully. "We got his bank account info off him—even the Swiss one." Terk flashed a grin. "And his bitcoin account."

At that, she snickered. "Well, all you need for that are the passwords, and anybody can take it over."

"Exactly. Where he's going, he won't use it anyway."

"I'm not even sure what happens when somebody with bitcoins dies. Does everything stay hidden in their account?" she asked.

"Pretty well, unless they've handed over the login information and password to move it."

"Which most of the guys like this don't because they're all superparanoid."

"This guy is a loner. He also has a cocky attitude, like he's invincible or something."

Celia nodded. "So I doubt that his affairs are in order."

"Well, if he's part of this whole bullshit mess," Terk declared, "I've got no problem taking the money to look after the babies. They're responsible for your condition. They should help take care of the expenses that are coming up."

"Exactly." She beamed. "So, when will you let me test you?"

"Never," Terk snapped, his voice clipped.

Her expression fell. "Why not?" she demanded.

"Because I already know what I can do. I'm not one of the ghost boys in your classes or your labs, who are wondering just what they can or cannot do." His gaze was hard. "I went through that stage with my team. I sure as hell don't need somebody else giving me some validation of it."

"I can see that," she said, her voice soft, "so maybe you can teach me to do more."

"Have you opened that pathway yet?"

She frowned. "No."

"Come find me when you do." And, with that, Terk turned and walked out.

Alfred whistled. "Wow, you two really do have relationship issues to resolve, don't you?"

"Like what?" she asked, turning to look at him in surprise. "If you mean a *relationship*-relationship, then you don't understand that there isn't one. He knows of my work, and here he can do all this stuff, but I don't even understand what he's doing. He was just pissed because I brought up testing again, which seems to be a sore subject."

Alfred looked at her with amusement. "It sounded like he seems to think you can do something, and he's given you a way."

"And he's wrong. I tried, … and it didn't work."

"Is that what you do with your students? You tell them to try once, and, if it doesn't work, walk away?"

She flushed. "Of course not," she muttered, "but this is not exactly the work I'm used to doing on the fly."

"I don't think it's the work you're used to doing at all, but you've got to understand this guy. Terk can do a lot, and, if you're looking to learn, he's the one to teach you. However, you have to match his pace."

She nodded. "Message received," she murmured. "He's just not easy to get along with."

"On the contrary, Terk is very easy to get along with," Merk said, as he walked in the room, having overheard the last part of the conversation. "You just have to understand where he's coming from."

"Then go along with his way, I presume."

He grinned at her. "Absolutely. Listen. None of us are exactly easy to be with around here," he said, with a wave of his arm. "This work that we do requires us to be very capable, decisive, confident, and very intolerant of fools."

She wasn't sure if that clipped note to his voice was directed at her or not. "I'm not a fool," she snapped.

"I never suggested that."

But it was not an apology he offered. All these guys were strictly no bullshit, and she knew it. It was probably her own insecurities making her feel so sensitive. And now she had already made it seem as if she wanted an apology for nothing. She groaned. "You do know this is not a very normal place."

"It sure isn't," he said, grinning, "and thank God for that."

She stared at him. "Do you have a partner?"

"Meaning that you can't see how anybody would possibly like me?" Merk asked, with real amusement in his voice and a wicked grin on his face.

"No, I wouldn't go quite that far," she protested. "Don't go putting words in my mouth."

"I'm not. But am I married? Hell yes. I'm married and very happy to be in that state. Sometimes you make mistakes in life, and sometimes you get a second chance."

"And sometimes you never get a chance," she murmured.

He looked at her, nodded. "Sometimes you have to take a chance to make something happen in your world." He nodded to the doorway, which she assumed meant toward his brother. "Life has just dealt you a very interesting hand of cards." He raised his eyebrows at her, his stare intense. "It's up to you to make whatever you can make out of it." At that, he was gone.

She noticed that Alfred was very studiously busy in his corner, like he was trying to stay out of the conversation or waiting for her to say something. She had nothing to say. She didn't have a clue what to say. That was the thing. These guys were so much more than anything she'd ever expected to come up against that she didn't know how to handle them. "Talk about being more alpha than anybody could deal with," she muttered to herself.

At that, she looked over her shoulder, and, out of the corner of her eye, she saw Alfred trying hard to contain his mirth. She grinned as she walked over, wrapped her arms around him, and gave him a huge hug. "You are allowed to laugh, you know?"

He cut loose with a great peal of laughter that made the whole kitchen light up. "Oh my," he said, still chuckling. "Thank you for that."

"For what?" she asked helplessly.

"For just being you." He turned around, gave her a nudge. "Maybe you should go lie down for a bit."

"Meaning, I should go practice some more?" she asked, with an eye roll.

"Whatever you think is best." Alfred gave her a bright smile. "It's not up to me to say what you need to do."

"You mean, you won't tell me to go practice on my own?"

He chuckled. "I think you know exactly what you need to do."

She did, though it was something she didn't really want to do, which was why it pissed her off. "Fine," she muttered.

"I don't know when I'll be down then."

"It's okay. I'm sure you'll be awake by the time dinner is ready."

"Maybe," she muttered, as she walked over to the fridge and snagged an apple, then walked out, leaving Alfred alone in the kitchen.

TERK HAD TO leave the kitchen immediately.

Being close to Celia was overwhelming, and even now he could still feel her presence. The fact that she was carrying his children was an aphrodisiac he had never anticipated. He didn't even know it was a thing, until something about the inherent femaleness of the whole pregnancy event hit him right in the groin, and he didn't have a clue how to handle it.

He climbed the stairs to his room, intent on taking a bit of a break. He had this ten-minute ritual where he let all the information slip through his brain. It was his way of sifting through data and retaining information. It really helped him, and, right about now, he needed to reevaluate and tightly dissect all the information from this prisoner.

The damn US government was involved.

It all came back to them, but Terk needed to know for sure. He needed to know what was going on and who was behind it. He didn't want that to be true, but, at this point in time, he was pretty damn sure Jerome was right about that.

Whoever had picked up that contract needed to be stopped, and then Terk still had to solve the government problem.

That would be a challenge.

He liked challenges.

Not like this though.

Yeah, not like this.

His thoughts raced at the speed of light. And the thought that his old bosses were involved was pissing him off.

As he laid here on the bed, his legs crossed at the ankles, while he stared up at the ceiling, he wondered what he could do or who he could contact for information, without setting off alarms that he was on to them.

He highly suspected that Bob—their contact at the defense department, who had been murdered—was part of it, and Terk thought about who Bob's boss was. Most of the time Terk and his team didn't have anything to do with them because the team just dealt with Bob. But now that Bob was gone, who would be in charge of the operations?

Did Terk have any loyal contacts left in the government?

He quickly sent Lorelei a text, asking her for the hierarchy of their old department.

She responded right away. **No hierarchy left. Department dismantled. Those left were moved to new jobs—like me.**

He replied, asking her to find out who it was before.

He wasn't sure how much digging she could do, but, other than that, he could put Tasha on it. She had some deep connections into their world. She didn't just do the job, she lived it, and, almost everywhere, she seemed to have people who owed her.

They needed those connections now more than ever. Maybe some were not necessarily the ones he needed right now, but Terk and his team needed something to jumpstart this investigation in the US government itself.

Later he tried to empty his mind to see what patterns would rise to the surface. He always found that same pattern every time he went into this dark place—one of betrayal. He didn't even know most of the bosses above him. He hadn't given a damn, as long as he had been left to operate autonomously, because it had all been functioning perfectly.

Until, … until they decided he was dangerous.

Terk frowned at that. Had somebody higher up convinced the government that Terk's team was too dangerous or was it some government body that came to the conclusion on its own?

Terk thought about all that they had seen coming out of Iran—the Iranian team being put together, much like his own team, and then the literally mind-shattering technology—and realized it wasn't even that simple revenge motive.

Definitely somebody on the inside of the US government was gunning for Terk's team. As for motivation, Terk was pretty sure that whoever it was, in that guy's mind, Terk's team was too powerful and had outlived their usefulness, and the guy was looking for an easy way out to be rid of Terk and his men.

What the government had thought of as an easy physical termination of Terk's team had turned out to be such a hot mess that they had no choice but to kill their own operatives, one after the other, who had failed to kill Terk's team, despite numerous attempts.

Terk didn't know everybody in the defense department or elsewhere in federal defense positions, but nobody in the government that Terk knew had struck him as particularly bright. While the people were beyond intelligent, uncanny, and master planners, they were never given the full accounting of Terk's team's capabilities. Terk always made sure to say no more than what was necessary.

As he lay here, emptying his mind, trying to find that peaceful center, where he could sort out information as it flowed his way, he felt energy coming toward him. He frowned because it was focused and steady, and, from what he could sense, there was absolutely no threat.

That made him wonder.

As it got closer, he realized it continued to head directly for him. He sat up in bed, watching what, to him, was almost a visible thread of white smoke approaching.

Seconds passed, and then it struck him hard.

"Now, isn't that clever," he murmured to himself as he studied it.

He closed his mind and reached out with his thoughts. *Now what will you do?* There was a gasp in his mind, as Celia connected, and he chuckled. *That wasn't particularly orthodox*, he murmured, *but I can see the energy.*

But I can't seem to connect it to you, she groaned in frustration.

After a moment of silence, he asked, *So then, what is it that you think you are doing now?* More silence came, then another gasp, followed by her peal of laughter that made him giddy.

It's really that easy, isn't it?

Yes and no, he replied. *When you sent that energy probe, I accepted the energy, so that we could communicate. I'm not sure what would happen if you utilized that methodology with somebody who didn't know how to do the connection on this side.*

Right, there's always a trick somewhere, isn't there?

I don't know about any trick, but always something needs to be done, one way or another.

Anchors do help though, she murmured, only her voice trailed away somewhere.

You can come across that same line into my thoughts whenever you wish. If you get there, and you can't get in, you'll probably find a door.

A door? So, in this case, the door was open?

Yes, I wanted it open, so you could get in. Now that you've got that accessibility, you'll also find that the door is closed a lot.

After a moment, she muttered, *Well, I'm learning.*

You are, indeed. He smiled, then deliberately closed the door. With that, he shut himself off from a very disturbing influence. The fact that she could now communicate with him just showed a glimpse of how gifted she truly was. That she affected him on so many other levels told him how dangerous she was to his control.

The fact that she studied abilities like his blew him away. He never considered that she'd be such a fast learner. But, of course, why wouldn't she be? Chances are, that's how she had ended up on everybody's radar.

Did they even know about the rest of her patients or subjects?

Was that something that he needed to worry about?

He contemplated that for a moment, and, rather than burning through energy, he picked up the phone and called her.

When she answered, she asked right away, "Where did you get my number?"

"I got it almost as soon as we arrived," he said calmly. "Communication is essential, and the question I have to ask you is also important. Think about the subjects in your scientific studies. Are there any who we need to be worried about?"

She gasped. "Oh my, I don't think so, but I didn't know that I was in danger to begin with, so how will I know?"

"Good point," he muttered. "Do you know if any of them have disappeared?"

"No, I don't. Remember. I completely dropped out of life when I was kidnapped. I'm out of the loop, and I don't have my files either. Also most likely I've been fired. I have no idea."

Trying to ignore the tightness in her voice, he asked, "Do you have online access?"

"I don't know. Would it be a simple matter to check? I don't want to lead anyone here."

"It would be simpler than you're likely thinking," Terk suggested. "Even an email or a phone call would let us know if they're available and in decent health."

"I didn't even consider that," she cried out, horrified. "Are they really in danger? I'd feel terrible if someone got hurt because of me."

"Well, we only just realized that it's probably because of your studies that you were brought into this. I hardly think you're to blame for that."

"But it feels like I am," she whispered. "I'll have Stone check them out and make sure, so it's not a total cluster fuck. I'll see if I can get Ice to bring up or give me safe access to my emails." She paused, then added, "I should have a backup of all my files too."

"Good enough. I'll come down and meet you there." He hopped up from the bed and headed to Ice's office suite. When he walked in, he saw Ice and Celia, both sitting at one computer.

Celia looked up, smiled. "I'm just logging in now."

"Good," he murmured.

Ice looked over at him impassively. "Do you think everybody's in danger?"

"I don't know whether she was picked as being the most skilled or one of a dozen chosen randomly."

At that, Ice winced. "I can't even bear thinking about that."

"No," Terk agreed, "but we already wondered if there are more gifted children within Celia's testing group to be kidnapped, so there could be more subjects to study by the kidnappers."

"Did the researchers run the subjects through a test to find out who might be the best? Or in some way try to evaluate the strength of their abilities?" Ice asked Celia.

Terk looked at Celia. "Did you have the test results on these people's abilities?"

With a sick look on her face, she nodded. "Yes, of course. Grants always have documentation and reporting required. The questions were fairly standard, and it all looked routine to me at the time."

"I get that, but say somebody else logged into your files or was already working with you and chose to sell that information for money. How would that be gathered? How secure were your files?"

"To the level you guys are used to? Not even close. And why would they be?" she asked. "I'm a scientist, not somebody dealing with online espionage."

"That's valuable to know too, in most careers," he said thoughtfully.

"Are you thinking that the others have been injured in some way?"

"No, not necessarily, but I think we need to contact them to see if they've had any strange dealings with anyone.

That would be a good start," he murmured. "Maybe they were contacted by this group."

"We do have some people here who could call," Ice suggested. "Or maybe I'll start calling everyone myself."

"And me," Celia said instantly. "I mean, they know me after all." As she quickly typed away on the computer, she brought up her email. "I always bcc my personal email address on every business email, thinking it was a fairly safe way to back up everything."

"It's not a bad way," he agreed, "unless somebody has access to either of your emails."

"I don't know anybody who would, but it's not as if any of this stuff has been terribly secret. I've already submitted papers to the journals with some of the results, which have been published by now."

"And did you name names?"

"Pseudonyms to protect their privacy."

"Well, that's something," he noted. "It could be that, because you're the one doing the studies, you were the one they targeted."

"Also," she confessed, "if anybody were to look into my history, they would see a little more than I would care to have out there."

"Meaning?"

"Meaning, I've assisted the police at times. Successfully so, I'm afraid." She shrugged. "It's not as if my abilities or the work that I've done has been a secret."

"Okay, that's worth looking at." Terk turned to fully face her. "What kind of police work?"

"Murders, and one particularly bad, ugly pedophile case."

"Those are nasty," Ice agreed. "Were you able to help?"

She nodded. "Yes, we managed to find him, and he was killed during the investigation."

"Interesting," Terk replied. "Another potential reason why you were picked too."

"Why? Because I help the police?"

"Do you know anything about the man's family? After all, he was convicted on paper but not in the courts."

She stared at him and swallowed. "Wow. All my actions suddenly have a long tail that I hadn't even considered."

"And unfortunately," Ice added, "we can only do our best each time, but we can never underestimate the people out there who don't choose to believe the truth, even when they see it or hear it. So, while the police may have been satisfied that he was the pedophile, his family might feel differently."

"Good Lord." Celia stared at Ice. "But would they really do something like this to me because they think I set up their loved one?"

"Oh, that's definitely possible." Ice nodded her head. "As much as we don't like it, an awful lot of people out there have agendas that don't align with everybody else's. A lot of times, their idea of fair play is nothing close to normal. Most people would blame the police, but others wouldn't be even that fair and would definitely blame you."

Celia didn't even know what to say to that.

CHAPTER 7

ICE'S WORDS HAD sent a chill over Celia's soul. "Somebody was staking out my house one night. One man was very aggressive and angry about my involvement with the case. He almost caught me and did tell me that I would pay. However, I think he's in jail still."

"Well, there you go," Ice said. "Even if it isn't the same guy who's doing this, you could have other enemies out there."

"Maybe, but how are *they* related?"

"Maybe they aren't," Terk replied. "Unless somehow the right person accidentally was looking for somebody with these kinds of skills, and they told them about you. Preferably hoping that you would be hurt by it all."

"Jesus." Celia stared at him. "I think I prefer the other versions, where we were working with a broader category of evil, instead of thinking this was a personal vendetta against me."

"The thing is, it could be anything," Terk said calmly. "Some potential reasons might feel better than others, but that fact is, we don't know and have to keep all options open."

She shook her head. "*You* have to. I'm not even sure I can deal with this anymore."

"Our choices are limited."

Her mind buzzed, as she thought about the ramifications of anybody involved in her studies being affected by this. But, at the same time, to think that any of the police work she'd tried to help with could come back to haunt her in such a way was also mind-boggling. And very disturbing.

In all cases, she'd only wanted to help people, but it seemed like her help, or her version of help, not only landed her in dangerous waters but also had ruined her life—potentially other lives too.

She quickly clicked through her emails, looking for the members' lists on the studies. "We didn't have very many in the program. The problem has always been trying to find people with a valid ability."

"Exactly," Terk agreed. "Honestly, it's been very hard for me to find qualified people to add to my team as well. We are a very select few, with very specific skills."

"Are all your test subjects male?" Ice asked.

"Yes," Celia replied.

"*Hmm.* So are my applicants," Terk noted. "I didn't think about this until just now, but two incredibly talented females with abilities declined my invitation to be part of my team some time ago," Terk said thoughtfully. "Yet they helped me get some team members through the terrible effects of the attack and the comas afterward, plus have now partnered with members on the team. I consider them part of our group. We also have Tasha, who was an admin, but was training to become a ground."

"Grounds are very important." Celia narrowed her gaze, as she asked, "Was this sexism on purpose?"

He shook his head. "No, my best opportunity to find candidates was to search through a large group from the military, who had already been well vetted in many aspects of the work, plus were skilled in warfare. So it stands to reason to check them first." He was honest about it and needed her to understand that. "Males dominate that field."

"You had a natural selection process available to you, which was a great asset," Celia noted. "Yet I really struggled to find people to test."

"And the fact that you found any is amazing," Terk replied.

Celia shrugged. "Not very many though. At the initial phase, I only had twelve."

He looked at her in surprise. "What do you mean when you say, *initial phase?*"

"Some dropped out. Some were proven to be less skillful than they thought they were, and some of them were just uncontrollable."

He nodded at that. "Did they need medication?"

"I was trying not to make those kinds of suggestions, but definitely a few instances came up where they were unstable—to the point of needing medication to even just keep their thoughts halfway straight." She looked from one to the other. "One of the sad facts of our shadow world is that, all too often, people with these kinds of abilities end up being diagnosed with severe dissociative disorders, like, schizophrenia or other even more complicated disorders." She looked at Terk. "I'm sure you found some of that yourself."

He nodded. "When I was looking within the military, even within that highly trained and able set of the best of the best, several people told me of their fear of being identified as freaks. Yet they were all solid, strong, and highly functioning in the real world. I didn't have to deal with finding people who didn't already know what they were up against."

"And were they all functioning on an energy level at the

time?" she asked in amazement.

"On one level or another," he confirmed, a note of amusement in his voice. "Whether they truly understood what they were doing or not, they had it together."

"You must have had some way of sorting them out." Celia studied Terk. And then it hit her. "You can see it," she cried out excitedly, as she pushed back her chair and raced over toward him. "You can see who has abilities."

He gave her a flat stare. "Can I?"

She cleared her throat. "You know how you expect me to open up to you? And here is an opportunity for you to open up to me as well." Her hands were fisted on her waist, as she leaned forward ever-so-slightly toward him, "I have been looking for ways to find out who is utilizing their energy in this way, so I could be trained to do this too. … That's what you did. … That's how you found out who you should select, isn't it? That's got to be it. It's the only scientific conclusion that works."

Terk shrugged nonchalantly and crossed his arms over his chest. "And?"

She almost glowed with excitement.

"It won't help you any," he pointed out coolly.

She glared at him. "I'll work on you."

He shrugged. "It won't change anything."

"It's already changed things," she declared in a hard tone. "It's a two-way street, Terk."

"But you're not on my team," he said in a smug voice.

With that, she gave him a haunted look. "If I'm not on your team, does that mean you're not on mine?"

TERK HADN'T MEANT the conversation to go that way, but he could understand the subtle difference in Celia's question. He immediately shook his head. "That's not what I meant."

"No. It's not what you meant, but maybe it's something you need to think about."

He saw the frustration in her energy, but underneath that was sadness and ... loneliness. Something that made him pause because he recognized that feeling well.

Celia added, "As I tried to point out, it's a two-way street, and that includes all directions. Particularly for people like us."

There was a lot of truth to what she said, but Terk wasn't happy about having been pinned in place. He also wasn't used to talking about stuff like this. It made him uncomfortable. He stiffened and raised an eyebrow. "I'll think about it."

"You need to think about it pretty damn fast"—she glared at him—"because I won't stick around and wait."

He crossed his arms and asked, "What does that mean?"

"You know perfectly well what it means, better than anybody else in this room," she snapped.

With that, he realized they had gotten quite an audience at that point in time. "Fine," he growled.

"No, it's not fine. You don't get to just back off like that." She continued. "You made it very clear that I'm not part of your team. So I need to know just where I do stand."

"You're not part of the *old* team, but, hell, that old team has already expanded to incorporate many new members. I'm not sure how anybody fits, except they are all family at this point. Considering you are carrying my twins, you are family too."

"And that brings up another point." Her gaze narrowed

again, as she stared at him. "I'm sure you're well aware of how abilities will change and grow, as more of you are living and working together."

He nodded slowly. "We have seen that synergy within the team unit, yes. It was amazing to see how everybody could learn and do so much more with the extra energy."

"And now you've just added new members," she stated, "so that growth will be exponential."

He nodded again. "It appears to be a possibility, yes."

She smiled. "And you're not exactly sure how you feel about that kind of change, *hmm?*"

"Does anybody ever handle it well?"

"Maybe not, but change is facing you right now, so you get to change with it or to be left in the dust."

"Well, that won't happen," he declared, glaring right back at her.

"Good," she murmured. "Not on my side either." And, with that, she walked back over and sat down at the computer.

He glanced at Ice.

Her gaze went from Celia to Terk, with something akin to astonishment written on her face. She looked at him and gave a helpless shrug, as if she only understood part of it.

Terk then realized just how much a gift it really was that Celia even understood what she had been spouting back at him.

He'd never met anyone like Cara and Clary either, who were phenomenally talented in so many ways. Celia hadn't had the benefit of others of her equal measure to advance her abilities, not as Terk's team had. It made Terk wonder what Celia could do if she did get that kind of assistance.

Because most civilians, even some of the military, had no

clue about myriad energy work. Sure, Cara and her sister Clary knew. Tasha knew, and by now Sophia and Lorelei did too, but holy Hannah. … Terk hadn't really expected to have somebody else stand up to him and push back at him, like Celia just had.

It was an unnerving experience, and he turned on his heel and walked out. He heard the silence echoing behind him and wasn't sure whether anybody would break it or wait until he was well out of earshot. As he headed toward the jail, he met Levi walking toward him in the hallway.

Levi looked at him and frowned. "You okay?"

"Yeah, I think so, but I find myself in an odd position. I think I just lost an argument for the first time in a very long time."

Levi raised his eyebrows, then burst out laughing. "Yeah, that would be between you and Celia, *huh?*"

Terk looked at him, amused. "Yes, I'm not exactly certain how it happened, but somehow she's part of my team."

"Of course she is," Levi replied, still chuckling. "She has abilities too. Something she hasn't utilized while she was here. I don't know whether that's a good or a bad thing, but I think she's used to keeping everything close to her chest. When she realized that you had similar skills, it stands to reason she would be more comfortable and more likely to express herself openly more and more."

"You have no idea."

"Well, that's not necessarily bad either," Levi admitted. "She's been getting stronger, gaining more self-confidence, and—with you here—a spine."

"It's a bit of a shock. I'm used to being the boss, and I'm sure you'll understand this. I am used to having people step up when I say step up. I am used to having people do what needs to be done, not necessarily because I told them to but because it needed to be done. But, in the case of the women on our team, it's a completely different ballgame."

"Yeah, it is." Levi's grin didn't diminish. If anything the wattage increased.

"I'm only just realizing that. I've always deliberately distanced myself from everybody outside of my team because of the dangers in my world," he shared, "but, as she just pointed out, I'm either on her team—and she's on mine—or neither of us is on the other's."

Levi blinked, as if trying to work through that convoluted message. After a moment, he nodded. "You know, Terk. She's right. Particularly since you both have these kinds of abilities. There is no option for distance in this. Your lives are now intertwined, and you won't untangle them for a long time, if ever."

"Assuming she gives birth safely and successfully, those children will be a part of me that I never thought I would have, and I'm not about to hand that off blindly."

"Good," Levi stated, "because I can tell you that fatherhood has brought some rather incredible feelings into my life. I never really expected to be a father, and I was hesitant about going in that direction because of our lifestyle, but my life is definitely richer for having them."

"Of course," Terk agreed. "And it's easy to see that in others, but it's a whole different story when trying to see it for yourself."

Levi slapped him on the shoulder. "Isn't that the truth?" He looked around and asked, "Where were you heading?"

"Down to see the prisoner."

"Any particular reason?"

"No." Terk shook his head. "That's where my feet were

leading me."

"Is that something you're supposed to let your feet just do?"

"Yeah, lots of times it works out pretty well for me."

"Good then. … Let's both go see the prisoner. Maybe he'll come up with something new. Maybe we can make this move forward."

"Waiting is always the worst. However, considering the next assault team is a few miles away, the wait will be short."

"A good ten miles," Levi corrected Terk.

"No." Terk stopped and stared out in the distance. "They're on the move, heading toward us right now."

Levi looked at him. "Shit. Do you still need to see the prisoner?"

"I do." But this time, he picked up the pace and raced down to stand outside the prison cell. He stared at the man for a long moment.

The prisoner gave him a lazy-eyed look. "Now what?"

Studying him, Terk could see the frayed nerves of the prisoner, as he glanced repetitiously at the clock.

"Yep, they're on the move," Terk said. "You'll be unprotected down here, you know? I'm not sure what your self-defense skills are like, but you might want to be prepared."

"Of course I'm prepared," Jerome snapped, "but they won't leave me. They'll bust me out of here in no time."

"They're not coming to rescue you."

"They're coming to take out all you guys, so call it whatever you want."

"Yeah, and we're ready." Terk waved his hand, completely dismissing the validity of the other man's words. "It's not like they'll succeed."

"You shouldn't be quite so cocky about it all."

"Why not?" he murmured. "We have absolutely no reason to worry. You saw for yourself this is a fortress."

"So why are you here checking on me?" Jerome asked.

"Just looking to see if I could get any other info from you."

At that, the other man's face turned thunderous. "I haven't forgotten all the shit you pulled before. That's bullshit. All of it, complete bullshit."

"Maybe. We'll have to see." Terk continued to peer at him, as if studying the man.

"See what?" he roared. "What are you doing?"

"I'm just looking, that's all. Just looking." Then Terk turned to Levi, impatiently waiting in the doorway, and smiled. "Don't worry about it," he told Levi. "Go on and get ready. He doesn't have anything to offer. He also doesn't know that he's the target and that they're coming here to put him down too."

"That won't happen," Jerome yelled.

Terk looked over at him, with a sad smile. "Sorry, but it's always the same. Much like you taking out those two you brought along. It's already in progress. The orders have been given. Somebody named *Bill* is coming in to take you out. So, when you see him, you might want to remember that."

"Bill wouldn't do that," he protested. "We're friends."

"Yeah, but he's the one who recruited you, and you've been taken prisoner, so he's not on your side anymore." Terk nodded slowly at the look of fear on the man's face. "Which means he's responsible for taking you out. He brought you on, and he's responsible for you doing the job. And, if he doesn't kill you, he's dead too."

"It won't happen." Jerome shook his head frantically. "We're friends. We've been friends since grade school."

"And I'm happy for you because obviously he's been somebody you've counted on all these years. Believe me. He's not looking forward to this, but, if he doesn't do it, he's a goner himself. So anyway, see ya." And, with that, Terk turned to leave.

CHAPTER 8

CELIA WAS BURNING through the phone calls, fast and furious.

She had to leave several messages, and, so far, had only connected with two of her test subjects. Neither reported anybody contacting them out of the blue. That was surprising, but then maybe not. They were very concerned about her disappearing out of the blue but appeared to accept her *car accident, then coma* excuse. By the time she'd finished, she was starving. She looked over at Ice and said, "Nothing."

"Good, and at least now they'll be on alert in case anybody does contact them."

"Do you think that's likely?"

"No, I really don't. I think the kidnappers—or whoever hired them—already have enough loose threads right now to control as it is."

"That makes sense in a sick way," she murmured.

At that, came an announcement on the PA. "Intruders on the move. Four miles out. Everybody to their stations."

At that, Ice turned to Celia. "Head on up to your room and lock yourself in."

Celia protested, "I should do something more."

"If you can do it on your own turf, something psychic, then be my guest, but this is nonnegotiable," Ice said in an uncompromising tone. "Go on. Protect your twins."

With absolutely no way to argue that, Celia headed up to her room. She passed Alfred on her way. "Will you go to your room too?"

"Nope, not yet," he said cheerfully. "I'll go get some weapons from the armory." She hesitated, and he shook his head, seeing the look on her face. "Don't even think about it. You're not trained."

"But I could be trained."

"If that training had happened in the last few months, then great, but it's too late now. Nobody is allowed a weapon who hasn't been fully trained, no matter what the situation. We are minutes from an attack, so now is not the time."

"Fine," she muttered and headed to her room. Once there, she locked the door as instructed and sat down. Knowing a full-on attack was coming was the most unnerving sensation. She looked around the room and realized she didn't even have a way out of this place. And that was a scary thought too.

What if somebody tried to burn down the place?

At that, Terk's voice popped into her head. *It's pretty fire-resistant. The building itself is made out of concrete. Plus a ventilation system keeps fresh air flowing. Believe me. They've been attacked more than once over time here, and this place is like Fort Knox. You are safest in your room, so stand by until it's over.*

What if I don't want to?

What surprised her was the laughter in his voice. *I don't want to come chasing after you to keep you locked in, but I will if I have to. Yet, if you pull me away from my post, then somebody else will have to cover for me, and we'll be spread too thin. So you need to do what you've been assigned, just like everybody else.*

You mean, stay out of the way.

No. I mean, stay safe and protect the babies.

"I can do that," she whispered.

He disappeared from her mind, and she sat down, everything inside her tense and nervous, as she waited in the darkness for the attack to come.

TERK SMILED, AS he quickly took up a position just inside the hidden corridor. She was learning and growing all the time. And he had to admit to admiring her grit. Hell, he was starting to like her too damn much. Still, he'd known from first seeing her what she was to him. Too bad if his mind was taking time to agree.

Everybody was spread all around the property, and all the cameras were live.

Stone was at his post in the control room. Ice was down in the armory, decking herself out, and even Alfred had pulled as much weaponry as he could get. As for Terk, he had other abilities and carried fewer guns.

His brother, however, was fully loaded, as were the few other people still in the compound.

Terk stood silently in the corner, sending out probes and looking for the attack points, trying to isolate where it could come from. He had a headset on for everybody's benefit. "Stone, check the satellite to the north, about two miles out."

"I got him," Stone snapped, his voice hard. "We've got four trucks inbound."

"Should be some ATVs coming cross-country as well."

Terk heard computer keys clicking in the background.

"Looking for them now," Stone confirmed. "Yep, I got two ATVs coming in hot. Both are loaded for bear."

"Well, let's hope they find bear then, preferably grizzly."

"Oh, they'll find a whole lot more than they expect," Stone said. "Anybody else you picking up on?"

"Yes, but …" Terk hesitated. "I don't know. I'm getting something strange, like a mechanical-human interface."

"Ah, you're right, a drone."

"Somebody is bringing the same tools that were used against us in France and England."

"Well, we've got drones here too." Stone spoke up, "Logan, you there on the comm?"

"I'm here," Logan confirmed. "I've got a drone setup as well. We're sending out two right now. Flynn's here with me."

"Good enough," Stone said. "I'll leave the drones to you, and I'll track them on our satellite as well."

"The security cameras should pick them up too," Levi suggested.

"Yeah, I've got them. We've got massive action happening here though."

"Yeah, they're all coming in at the same time and trying to overwhelm us," Levi agreed. "It's almost like some of our training scenarios, so we've seen it all played out before."

"But there's a big difference this time," Merk said, his voice calm in their ears. "Terk's here. And I know some of you probably don't believe the stories I've told you, but he doesn't even need that gun he's packing."

"Maybe not," Terk said, "but I can't take them all down at once, so everybody has a part to play."

"And will Celia stay locked up?"

"Well, she will for the moment," he said. "I can't tell you what will happen, depending on how long this goes on. But, for the moment, she trusts that we'll do all we can."

"And that's all any of us can do," Ice piped up. "And, while this isn't a practice run by any means, it is a training session of sorts. So we need to keep an eye toward how we can improve on the next one."

Terk grinned. "That was pure Ice, always looking for a way to make things happen. I do love that about you," he said in a teasing voice. "Not too many women would be strategizing on how to use the impending attack to improve our defensive response for next time the facility is under siege."

Levi snorted audibly, enjoying the joke.

"Yeah, you can trust Ice for that," Stone agreed, a note of admiration in his voice, marked with a note of surliness. "She'll have my head if I miss somebody."

"No I won't, but you know how I feel. We were considering putting two people in that room at all times anyway."

"Not at all times, but, yeah, I can see the advantage sometimes," he grumbled.

At that, Terk felt Celia pop into his head. *I can help too. I have eyes, even if I can't do anything else in this fight.*

Well, if you want. Out loud for everyone to hear, he said, "Celia just suggested that she could go help Stone. She's feeling pretty caged and quite pissed off that she's been relegated to the *little woman* role."

At that, Ice burst out laughing. "Well, if she had any weapons training, she'd be in position right now."

"For that matter," Stone said, "if she wants to come down and keep an eye on one of the monitors, I won't say no."

"Okay, then prepare for that," Terk said, "because I'm telling her now."

"How are you doing that?" he asked.

"You sure you want to know?"

"Oh, shit, man. More of that woo-woo stuff? No, I definitely don't want to know." Stone snorted. "But she'll have to give the password at the door because I'm not opening it otherwise."

"Right, let me relay the message. But sometimes it gets a little garbled, so have a little tolerance when she gets to the door." At that, Terk sent Celia a message, and she shrieked with joy.

I'm on the way.

Wait a second, Celia. You won't be let into that room, if you don't have the password.

And how will I get it? she asked.

I'll give it to you, but I need you to be calm enough to get it correctly.

Fine. Are there any booby traps on the outside that I should know of? she asked suspiciously.

Not that I know of. Then he said into his headset, "She wants to know if the door is booby-trapped, in case she gets it wrong."

"Not booby-trapped, but it still won't open until she gets it right."

"Noted," Terk said, and he passed that on. He waited until he heard her in his mind, as she tested the door. And suddenly Celia was speaking to Stone.

She said, "Well, look at that. Did Terk talk to you telepathically as well? We can work on training you."

"Oh, hell no," Stone snapped. "I like things black-and-white, things I can see, ... not things that go bump in the night."

"Who the hell are you to dismiss things that go bump in the night?" she asked. "All you do is deal with those things."

With that, Terk lost contact, as he closed the door in his mind and had to focus on what was happening right in front of him. "For all of you, Celia's in the control room."

"Good enough," Ice said. "I know that will make her feel better."

"One mile and counting," Terk added.

"One mile out," Stone repeated. "Dammit, Terk. I am supposed to be the lead on intel here," Stone grumbled.

"Sorry, but I was just waiting, and you were … a little slow," he replied, with a smirk.

"I'll give you slow," Stone growled, but then his voice shifted to all business. "We have one vehicle stopping one mile out, and one vehicle coming up to the front gate. That second one is going around the corner and parking. I've activated the security at the gate, so let's see what they do with that."

"Considered they put C-4 on Celia, I suspect it's a bomb," Ice noted.

"Well, in that case," Levi growled, "you better bring up the steel net."

And that's exactly what they did. Terk could imagine it happening in his head, but he couldn't see it, and that was too damn bad because the actual security on this place was beyond impressive.

He and Merk had helped set it up and had offered advice on what was the best, along with Bullard. The fact that Bullard wasn't here crossed Terk's mind. He asked Levi.

Levi laughed. "Believe me. He'd be here, if I'd have let him."

"You stopped him?"

"Yep, his wife's pregnant."

"She needed him home," Ice added. "She's nine months in."

"Holy crap," Terk said, "seems like everybody is in the reproductive zone."

"Including you, remember that," Ice snapped back hastily.

Just then, a huge explosion blasted outside.

Stone announced, "The net caught that one, but it's damaged. I'm bringing up the backup. Success will depend on how much firepower these guys have." Stone's voice was calm and steady. "We'll need bigger nets."

"We've already got a double net," Ice stated. "Who would have thought we'd need more?"

"Still not sure we do," Stone agreed, "but the dynamite will make a disaster of the cement wall outside."

"We can reinforce it later," Ice snapped. "I'm pissed they are getting this far."

"Just a consideration for the future, as requested," Stone said calmly. "They only came with one vehicle, so they must have a bunch of C-4. Somebody is already trying to hop out of the vehicle and is running toward the gate. Looks like they're expecting this next blast to give them entrance."

"I hope it does," Terk noted. "Because I'm already sliding out to help."

"You've got the one vehicle," Stone added, "parked just up and around the bend."

"Don't you worry," Terk stated, grinning. "That one's mine, you guys. Over and out. Happy hunting."

And, with that, he shut off all communication and went silent. Then he walked through the tunnel, his senses open, as he waited to see what kind of offensive onslaught he may be hit with. But it was quiet out there, very quiet. Then he realized that there might be another weapon that would be even harder to deal with.

It could be the same weapon, the mind-shatterer that had wiped out the team in the first place. And he had absolutely nobody to contact about it because it would only affect him.

Swearing at that, he raced down the tunnel and slid outside into the darkness. Then sent a message to his team in England. "Not sure where you guys are, but be warned. ... Looks like these intruders are reenacting the same attempt here in Texas that they did with their first attack on the team. Only this time with much more power."

He saw the vehicle up ahead. Something powerful hummed inside. He knew he had to get there and disable it fast, before it all blew up in more ways than one. And while he still had senses to even go with. Because, once that machine went off, it would be bad for his team, Celia, and, even more so, for him.

CHAPTER 9

A S CELIA SLIPPED inside the control room, she gasped as she stared around. "Good God," she whispered. "I would have expected to see something like this in a top-secret government facility, not here."

"We're basically a top-secret government facility," Stone joked. "And, even with all this, we still don't have a lot."

"Of course not." Celia shook her head. "Yet an incredible amount of equipment is here to keep your eye on though."

"There is. So catch your breath, and I'll give you a quick orientation to the room, and then we'll get you started." After a quick overview of the secure facility space, he said, "I'll give you a couple monitors to keep your eyes on."

She obediently sat down in the spare chair. "Okay, which ones?"

He pointed them out. "That is the north field. We have cameras and surveillance all over there. You will see Terk pop up somewhere along there."

"Is that where he is?" she asked.

Stone nodded, then laughed. "He's taking the north side because no way he won't be out there, and we need the manpower."

She agreed with that, but it was still hard to see just how much damage was going on. "Is it always like this?"

"Is what always like this?" He looked at her in confusion. "Your life."

"No, not at all, but, when it happens, you have to be prepared."

"You guys must have a lot of enemies."

"We do," he confirmed cheerfully. "And they're all assholes, so I don't worry about it."

"Until something bad happens to one of you guys."

"Or to one of Terk's team or to other friends of ours … in Bullard's group. Both of them have had major attacks on their teams. And we've been in the unfortunate position of having to help from the outside, all the while knowing it could always be us."

She shivered at that. "That sounds seriously depressing."

He chuckled. "Maybe, but we also have to live regular lives, and, for that, we've all moved forward with our personal lives, trying to get as much joy out of life as possible."

"I think somebody said you were married."

"Yep, I certainly am." Then he flashed her a grin. "Nope, I didn't suspect that would happen."

She shook her head. "I couldn't have foreseen what happened to me either."

"No, I don't think most people would have, but, when you consider what Terk can do, I'm surprised that some asshole didn't dream this up earlier. And between the abilities of the two of you, it makes sense somebody tried this, as terrible as it seems. And we still don't know how far they've gone."

"It's just wrong," she cried out, glaring at him.

He shrugged. "Absolutely, it's terribly wrong, but that doesn't change the fact that it's happening."

"But there is also no guarantee the children will even have any abilities. Look at Terk, yet his brother can't do any of that." Celia paused. "Merk did say he doesn't have the same ability, although I'm not convinced."

He looked at her, frowning.

Celia self-corrected. "Okay, let's just say that Merk has never shown that he has any of those abilities, which is a completely different story."

Stone acknowledged that difference with a head nod.

Celia added, "And just because he says that, you all believe him. What if it's just not something he's developed?"

"I don't know how any of that works, and I'm not sure I want to. I don't like what I can't see."

"Right, and that's understandable." As she spoke, she kept her eyes constantly focused on the two monitors he had assigned her, and he continually scanned other monitors and various equipment in the room. "In my work, I have found multiple people with some pretty major skills that weren't developed."

"And then what are you supposed to do?" He shrugged. "Not everybody wants to have these skills either, I'll bet."

"Right, and I have seen that as well." She paused. "I've had a few in my program who were pretty adamant about not having the skills that I could plainly see they possessed."

"And did you honor their opinion?"

"Absolutely, because there are also people who did have skills and thought they could do much more, yet couldn't control any of it. They ended up turning to substance abuse in order to dull the effects of what they were experiencing."

"Yeah, I can see that too. If you don't understand what's happening, I can imagine that it's terribly frightening. So dulling that with drugs or alcohol is probably quite a predictable response."

"Unfortunately that is true."

"So, you didn't have the same kind of reaction or what?"

"When I hit puberty, it was as if a floodgate opened. And things that I had always considered quite normal, I then found out were not normal at all. I quickly learned that I could do so much more," she murmured, "but people were put off by it, and I lost a ton of friends, before I figured it out and learned to keep my mouth shut."

He snorted. "Yeah, that should be like the first life lesson for all of us, no matter what we do, right? Keep your mouth shut, until you know who you can trust."

"And, of course, those people are few and far between," she murmured. "I thought my best friend was somebody I could trust, but she got drunk one night at a party and told everybody that I could do all these fun tricks. Then, when I wouldn't do them, she basically left me behind because I wouldn't do the party tricks, and she chose not to forgive me for that."

Stone snorted at that. "You see? That's the thing about people, and, until you're in these situations, you don't know what they'll do for or against you. They say that they're for you, but, as it turns out, they only want you around when it suits them. They want somebody they can trust, who stands with them in those kinds of circumstances, when the friendship is put to the test. You did the best that you could, and, as you said, life isn't always that easy."

"Not only not that easy, it can be seriously stressful."

"Absolutely," he murmured. At that, he stopped speaking and studied the monitor.

She looked over at him. "That look means you're seeing something, but I don't know what it means."

"And by the time I explained it, I already need to be on the move, doing what I need to do."

And, with that, he tapped on a headset in his ear, and she realized that he was wired and connected to the others. She watched in fascination as he adjusted dials and spoke into the headset.

"Terk, that truck," Stone said, "I'm not sure what they've got, but I see four men."

"Roger that," Terk noted calmly, his voice filling the room. "I think what they have is the same instrument that took out my team. The mind-shatterer."

"Well, that sucks," Stone replied. "Is it really something that's movable?"

"We never saw it, so I can't tell you that."

"I did get an update, and apparently your team is on the way."

"Of course they are," Terk said. "They won't be in time to do any good though, which I'm just as glad for, since they can't be hurt by the device if they're not here."

"Copy that," Stone replied. "I've got an eye on you. Don't do anything stupid. We need to make sure that machine is nullified somehow. I'll send backup your way."

"No, don't do it right now. I might be one of the few people who has a way to stop this thing from hurting me. I'm the only one who was still standing last time." Terk hesitated and then added, "And, Stone, because this machine is here, you need to make sure you keep Celia there. She's likely to be affected by it."

She frowned at that. When Stone got off, she asked, "What exactly does this thing do?"

"His entire team was taken out by this thing. Their abilities knocked out by some machine. They were comatose,

143

some for a long time, and God only knows how they even survived."

"*Great*. In that case, we're probably talking an EMP."

"Why do you say that?"

"Because not a whole lot else works on energy."

"Is that common knowledge?"

She shrugged. "I did a study on it at one time, but it was a long time ago, and it wasn't exactly a large project. We had about six of us, and it definitely did knock us out." She hesitated, then thought about it. "Honestly, we were out for a few days, but it wasn't horrific. However, we were using a pretty minor pulsing mechanism."

"*Minor* is not necessarily what this will be. If they're trying to take out Terk, and they know you're here, which of course they do since they're the ones who dropped you outside our gates, they're probably trying to take you out too."

"Are they expecting everybody else here to have the same abilities?"

"I wouldn't be at all surprised if they aren't concerned about that fact because Levi and Ice have a very strong program here and a really high success rate at everything they take on. Of course they're smart enough to only take on things that they know they can handle and complete. Not everybody will do that because the money is good." Stone grinned. "So their success rate is partly due to the judicious process they use to determine what jobs to take on."

"Right," she murmured. "And that can't be easy."

"No, we've had cases where people have come back against us because we chose not to take on a job. Then, when someone was killed, they blamed Levi for it."

"That's hardly fair." Celia glanced at Stone. "I mean, not

everyone can help everybody."

"Exactly, and, as long as you realize that, then—when the shit hits the fan—it makes it a little easier."

She groaned. "Meaning that Terk may not be able to help me."

"And that you may not be able to help him either. You must recognize your—and his—limits. You need to be aware of that."

"Of course. If these assholes have the ability to make something much bigger, much more powerful," she said, "then presumably they must have something in reserve to run it, versus that small vehicle."

He looked at her, impressed. "You mean, like, generators or a backup power supply?"

"I would think so." She frowned in consideration. "We didn't have much in terms of funding for our program because nobody, except me in a way, was concerned about how to knock out something like this. And my interest was more of a self-defense idea." He turned and looked at her. She stared at him, shaking her head already. "Oh, God, no, damn it. I don't want to hear that."

"You might not want to hear it, but that doesn't mean that isn't what happened."

"God, that would be absolutely terrible," she cried out.

"You apparently have hit somebody's radar, and some of the studies or work that you've been doing has made you a person of interest."

"Crap." She thought about the study they had been involved in. "We did find one way to help mitigate the damage, but honestly it was not even foolproof. One person managed to limit the effects, but there was still damage."

"What damage and how strong a level of damage?"

"Blackout effects but, in a situation like this, if an attack is underway, they would still be vulnerable."

At that, Terk's voice popped into her head. *Did I just hear something about an EMP test you did?*

"Yes," she said out loud and explained. "But honestly, it was minor."

Maybe minor, but what are the chances you gave somebody that idea?

"I don't know," she cried out in frustration. Only then she realized that Stone was looking at her weirdly. "Oh, shit." Celia scrubbed her face. "Stone is looking at me like I'm nuts."

That's fine. Terk laughed. *Stone is used to it.*

She looked over at Stone. "Terk says you've looked at him like he's nuts too."

Stone cracked a smile. "Yeah, but I hadn't really considered what it looks like when somebody else was doing it."

She glared at him. "The same. … I'm nuts too. In case you hadn't figured that out."

"Oh, I got it all right," he said, laughing. "Absolutely got it. What I hadn't really thought about was the possibility of there being more people like him."

"Well, there is at least me and his team. You know his team, don't you?"

"I know lots of them. We've certainly worked with a bunch of them."

"Well, it's no different than working with me," she said in exasperation. "I mean, I want to say we're … *special.*"

Stone nodded. "Definitely special," he agreed calmly. "And I don't think you guys realize even how special."

She heard Terk muttering in the background. "Talk to me," she said, "but you'll have to stop muttering."

He snorted. *What's the point of trying to talk to you, when you're busy talking to Stone?*

"Well, if you want me to not talk to Stone, you could have said something. I'm not used to this weird conversation that goes back and forth on two channels."

No, of course not, and I apologize.

She stopped and stared at Stone. "I don't think I've ever heard you apologize, Terk."

Stone just shook his head and ignored her seemingly one-sided conversation.

It's not as if you know me, Terk said in exasperation. *So I promise that I do apologize when necessary.*

"Back to the study, I mean, sure people saw the published papers, no doubt. Maybe some people found my research, or maybe it fell into the wrong hands. Maybe somebody did a search on EMP and psychics, then found my published study. I don't know. It's possible. ... I really can't say. We were trying to get grant money to continue those studies, and, of course, that was impossible. Everybody was talking about it being woo-woo stuff that couldn't be proved."

And who funded the first one?

"Honestly, I did," she admitted, "which is why I'm always broke because I'm forever testing my own research."

And that's a smart thing to do, Terk noted, *but publishing the results wasn't.*

"Thanks for that," she snapped. "You do realize that, in order to get grant money, you have to give them some kind of results. I had to do something in order to get more money to continue the research."

But it didn't work to generate any research funding, right?

"No, it didn't work," she snapped, glaring at the monitors in front of her. "But I'm not sure that truck could hold enough equipment to give you the powerful blast that it needs."

"Unless it's drawing power from somewhere else," he murmured, but this time he spoke through his headset *and* telepathically.

Stone started talking. "Yeah, I hear you, Terk. I'm not exactly sure that anybody could connect to a satellite for something like that."

"But the fact is, *we* are connected," Terk noted. "If they could tap into our power source, then potentially that would give them enough."

Stone looked over at her, and she nodded slowly. "I don't know what would be required on a large range scale. That's not my area of expertise."

She was glad that she had been allowed in here. The fact that she might have something to offer hadn't even occurred to her, but she was grateful that she could. And she had felt so disassociated from all this, until Terk's arrival. Back then the pregnancy hadn't felt real, until the babies started kicking, and then it was all too real.

Not knowing what the hell had happened to her life had sent her into a spiral of depression, but now? … Now, she had a direction.

She had a purpose now, and the fact that she might have contributed to this entire nightmare—unwillingly through her own work—was something that would take her a long time to resolve. Whether she had indirectly been part of the attack against him or not, she hadn't known anything about it, and she certainly hadn't played an active role. She wondered if Terk could even ignore and get past that.

Having connected with Terk's energy, there was just that

sense of surety about her place here. She was not quite willing to acknowledge that he was definitely the father but willing to consider that he could be. And that in itself was a huge step all on its own.

Her head spinning, she glanced up at the monitors and tapped it again. "Oh my," she said, nudging Stone. "I don't know what this is."

He hopped over to take a closer look. "Yeah, definitely a problem." He tapped his headset. "Terk, we've got the four men now out the other side of that truck."

"What are you thinking?"

"I'm not sure, but I think they're trying to protect it."

"That would make a sick sense in a way too," Terk murmured.

Stone added, "If this is superimportant to them, they must protect it."

"Of course they do, but, at the same time, we also don't want anything to go *boom* in the night."

"No, we don't," Stone murmured calmly. "And there have been an awful lot of booms in the nights lately."

"Here?" Terk asked, his voice sharp.

"No, nothing new, nothing recent. You already know about all of it from the past."

"I won't approach," Terk replied, "until we sort out where they're going."

"I've got two of our men coming to you. Logan and Flynn are both out there. Both with drones."

"Okay, give them my position and have them join me."

"Already done. Sit tight. We're on this."

"Yeah, I know you're on it. I just don't want anybody hurt."

"No, neither do we." And, with that, Stone signed off.

149

He looked over at her. "He'll be okay. You don't have to worry."

She only now noted that her fingers were clenched together so tightly that crescent-moon indentations were left on her palms. She shook her hands out and whispered, "I'm just not used to this."

"Nobody gets used to this," he murmured. "Just keep doing what you're doing, and it'll be fine."

She wasn't so sure, but she could do nothing else but sit tight and hope that this all worked out.

One thing she did know was that this situation was definitely outside of her experience, and chances are the rest of this entire chaos would be as well.

TERK WAS HAPPY to have the backup but still felt out of place without his team. Yet it was always good to know he was covered. The two teams had helped each other on cases before, but this would be something none of them were cut out for.

His team, Terk's team, he knew was definitely cut out for this. Being the people they were, with the abilities they had, it was easier.

He studied the four intruders, watching as they separated, with two heading out to the far side. Those two had now split, one heading south and the other east. Terk could no longer see them.

And they left the truck with the other two, who were obviously heavily armed. However, as the one walked forward, he kept looking back at the vehicle, as if not sure that it was safe to leave it behind. Of course the answer was hell no. It wasn't safe to leave behind.

The minute Terk could get down there, he would move that sucker a long way away. He just didn't exactly know what was going on inside the vehicle. And that would be an issue. If there was any way to immobilize the humming device within the truck, he'd do that too.

At that, he checked his pockets, though he knew he didn't have it. Damn, he should have grabbed some C-4. And, should he get a chance to put that in the vehicle and blow it to smithereens, he would. Levi might have to give some explanations to the local authorities, but Terk wouldn't worry about that now. Not his problem.

He almost laughed at his own thought because, of course, it *was* his problem. He wouldn't do that to Levi, but he also knew that Levi had an awful lot of pull when it came to shit like that around here. But who knew that they would need C-4 tonight, like they quite possibly could.

Terk worked his way closer, waiting to see what the two men heading in his direction would do. When Terk heard Stone in his ear, Terk pinpointed Flynn and Logan. He confirmed over the radio with Stone. Then, with them both nailed down, Terk watched as the two men from the truck approached.

Both intruders were heading in the direction where Flynn and Logan were, probably tracking them by the launch of their drones. Terk had seen the drones in the air, but both were likely damaged now, after taking out the other drones. Ice wouldn't love that. But if they'd done the job ...

Hearing a *clunk* off to the left, he acknowledged that Logan had taken one of them down. He waited for Flynn to take out the other one. It was a hair louder but not by much.

At that, Terk slipped forward and headed toward the

truck, trying to keep out of sight of the other two men. He had to assume they had comms, and, with the other two down, he knew the remaining two would find out something was up and would circle back soon.

At the truck, he tried to open up the big camper-size cover to the bed, where somebody could pile up their shit. It was locked. It took him only seconds to pick the lock and to open the door. He slipped inside, then, closing the door behind him, he turned on his flashlight. His heart froze. "Some machine is in here, and it is rumbling," Terk reported via his headset.

He had no clue what it was, so he immediately snapped photos of what he could see and sent them to Stone. Then, as an afterthought, he sent them to Celia's phone.

She responded in his head, saying, *I have no clue what that is.*

He asked, *Is it anything similar to the EMP system you had?*

No, not at all, nothing like that. Definitely not anything that big.

And yet you still managed to knock out abilities?

Yes, assuming these machines are the same, we used a lighter and smaller variation of this before, and it took several weeks for some of my team to come back online.

Stone was again in Terk's ear, telling him that his team was on its way here.

He swore at that. "Damn. And that just means they're back in the line of danger again."

Can you stop them? Celia asked.

I don't think anything will stop them at this point, he said, with a fatalistic tone that said he was used to dealing with some facts that just weren't helpful. *But still I can't put them in danger again. I'm warning them right now.*

What happens when shit hits the fan for you? she asked.

Just don't be surprised.

And, with that, he disappeared from her mind and her screen. At the vehicle, he checked underneath and all around it, knowing that he was in danger of being seen, but, at the same time, he didn't want them to turn this sucker on or to do something with it that would knock out anybody.

Finding wires, he started snipping. He saw no C-4, but that didn't mean that this vehicle wouldn't be wired to explode. He had only his instincts. And, with snippers in hand, he studied the wires. Black or yellow? He sent Stone a message. "Black or yellow?"

"Jesus, man, don't just do it haphazardly. You'll blow yourself up."

"I didn't see any explosives on the vehicle. And I've got the tester with me, and there's nothing in the vicinity."

"So, what is it then?"

"I don't know," Terk said, "but I'm very afraid that, if anybody finds out that I'm in here, they'll turn it on, and I'm the one who'll get fried."

"Absolutely you'll get fried," Stone said in outrage, "but I'm not sure how to stop it."

"The only other option is to blow up the truck," Terk stated.

"Well, you've got Logan out there. He's carrying C-4. It won't take very much to take care of the truck, and then they won't have the weapon either."

Terk contemplated that, and just then he sensed an energy approaching. "Check on the satellite. Somebody is coming."

"I can't see anybody," Stone replied.

"I don't care if you can see him or not," Terk replied in a soft voice. "He's coming. You need to find him."

At that, Stone swore. "Yeah, he's coming all right, and he's completely camouflaged. Couldn't see him on the satellite, but I got him now."

"How close to the truck is he?" Terk stared at the truck's back door.

"Too damn close. You can't get out now."

"No, I can't. That's probably what they want. Chances are they'll lock me inside and turn on this sucker."

"Don't worry," Stone said. "Flynn and Logan are heading toward you. Logan is handling the drone. The enemy drones have been decommissioned. If he has firepower on his drone, he's welcome to cut down the numbers."

"Which means," Terk noted, "these local footmen are just caught up in this part of the plan. I wonder if these intruders know that they're so disposable."

"Is that what you think is happening here with Camo Guy?"

"Yep, I think the foot soldiers came to do a job. They were probably fed a line about what it was they were supposed to do, and, now that they're off doing it, they have no idea that they'll get taken down. They may not even know what's in this truck. Now somebody else that they weren't expecting is here—Camo Guy."

"Are people really that stupid?" Stone asked.

"Lots of guys do things for what they think are the right reasons but don't realize how wrong they actually are."

"I hear you. We do have Camo Guy coming up on the truck right now though. He's just reaching for the door."

"Yep, I got it," Terk muttered. Tuning Stone out, Terk waited just a fraction of a second more, and then, with a strong right kick, he slammed the door open into the guy's face. He jumped down, as Camo Guy scrambled to get up, while pointing a handgun right at him.

Terk smiled at him. "What's the matter?" Terk asked. "You can't do this man to man?"

"I'm not such a fool. They say you have all kinds of abilities." He bounced to his feet, staring at Terk warily.

"Who? Me?" Terk acted surprised. "You don't even know who I am."

"Yeah? Well, your face was given to everybody on this team."

"What about the guys you sent out ahead of you?"

He smirked at that. "Well, maybe we didn't share that with them."

"So you know that you're all going to die on this mission, right?"

"Only if you guys are assholes."

"Because you're entering private property and carrying weapons in an obvious attempt to harm people on the property," he said gently. "That kind of thing will get a guy shot. And we're the kind of people who don't pick up a weapon unless we intend to use it."

"Yeah, well, I'm the same." He grinned. "And remember who's got the weapon on you."

"I see it." Terk gave a negligent shrug. "It's not like you are ever going to use it though."

"What the hell, man? You think you're better than me?" he mocked. "I'll shoot you where you stand."

"No, you won't. I'm sure you'd like to, but that gun won't fire."

The gunman raised his gun. "Do you see this? I'm more than happy to use it, asshole." Angrily, he pointed it at

Terk's knee and pulled the trigger. To his astonishment, nothing happened. He stared at him and then glared at the gun in his hand. "What the fuck?"

"I told you. It won't fire."

"You think I'm an idiot?" The guy looked at his gun and started pulling the trigger several times, but nothing happened. "What the hell? You couldn't have done anything because you never touched it." He was well beyond pissed over the whole scenario, but he braced himself and said, "Fine, I'll do it the old-fashioned way."

"Yeah, let me know how that works out for you." Terk laughed.

The guy roared and charged. Terk stepped to the side but wrapped an energy band around his feet and pulled upward. The guy immediately tripped and fell to the ground. He couldn't even separate his legs. Terk, with one hard punch to the jaw, knocked him out. "Stone, he's down. Send in the reinforcements."

"Both Logan and Flynn heading your way," Stone replied. "What the hell was that with the gun?" There was something in his voice.

Terk snorted. "What? Couldn't you see? It didn't fire."

"Yeah, I know it didn't fire," Stone snapped, "but shit, man, if you've got tricks like that, I want to know how it works."

"Oh no, you don't want anything to do with the boogeyman, remember? You like things black-and-white. Things you can see."

"Yeah. Well, I also would like to know how the hell you did that. If I'm up against a gunman again, I would like to take care of him, just like that. Hell, you don't even need the weapon in your hand."

"I do, depending on the distance," he said, as he reached into his back pocket and pulled out zip ties.

"Oh, come on. Who brings zip ties to a gun fight, for crying out loud?"

Terk shrugged. "I knew I would need them. Listen though. Keep an eye on Levi right now. Somebody is sneaking up on him."

"On it."

"And I'm bringing this guy," Terk said.

"I thought you were waiting for backup?"

"They're almost here, so we'll be over to help Levi in a few minutes." And, with that, Terk turned to face Flynn and Logan, who were looking at him and wanting an explanation. "This is the one who was hiding whatever is in that truck." He motioned at them to take a look.

They opened the door and whistled. "What the hell is that?"

"I don't know, but, if you've got C-4, I'd suggest we blow it."

"I'm all for that," Logan said, "but do we know it won't set off a bigger charge?"

"We don't know, though I tested for explosives. But, if that's a weapon specifically to be used against me, I'd just as soon we not give it a chance. My team is coming, and I want to make sure that they're safe too."

Flynn hesitated and then raised his palms. "Seriously? Blow it up? What if we can learn from it?"

"We can always learn from a close call too," Terk said in a hard tone. "Yet that doesn't mean it'll be a lesson I want to learn."

"You really think it's a weapon against you?"

"I know they had a weapon that they discharged before.

It took out my whole team, and, if this is it, or even related in any way, I don't want it operable."

"Maybe not, but wouldn't you rather know how they made it, so you could counter it down the road?" Flynn asked.

Terk glared at him because, in spite of Terk's uneasiness, that made sense. All he wanted to do was not be put out of commission. "If you can find a way to knock it out without turning it on, I'd say go ahead, but we don't have that ability yet. So the best answer is to just take it out of commission."

"Sure, but do we have to blow it up?" Flynn asked, looking at him, "Isn't there another way?"

"I don't know of another way," Terk snapped, "because I don't know how it works."

"Got it," Flynn murmured, as he studied the insides.

"Obviously it's got a container, and there's no ticking time bomb on it, but that doesn't mean that somebody from a distance can't turn it on remotely," Terk snapped. "So kill it."

"Right." Flynn winced at that, looking back at Logan. "As much as I'd like to keep it, I understand Terk's point."

Logan said, "What if it's just one of multiples?"

"Then we have to track them down," Terk said instantly. "I don't even want to think about that, but this one needs to be destroyed." And, with that, Terk looked at them and asked, "Now, will you do it, or will I?"

"I'll do it." Logan walked around to see all sides of the truck and got to work. After a few minutes he added, "It's also a nice truck."

"Don't care what it is," Terk snapped. "It's completely wired to whatever this thing is." And, with that, they backed away, and Logan set off the detonator.

CHAPTER 10

*B*OOM.

"Holy crap," Celia cried out. "What the hell was that?'

"I presume they detonated the truck carting the EMP," Stone said, tapping the far corner of her monitor.

She watched as a plume of smoke filled the air. "But how do we know if they're okay?"

Almost instantly Terk's voice filled her head. *I'm fine. We all are. It looked like an EMP weapon, and I wanted to make sure it was taken out.*

She agreed totally but wished there had been a little bit of warning. *You just took ten years off my life.*

Well, it would have been a lot more than that, Terk replied, *if this thing had gone off.*

Do you really think that's what it was? I think we should have studied it, so we could learn from it.

Sure, he said, laughing. *You're welcome to come pick up the pieces and study them all you want.* And, with that, he vacated her mind.

She glared at Stone. "Did you know how arrogant he is?"

Stone looked at her. "If you are talking about Terk, then, no, I didn't, but I'm sure you're about to tell me."

She fisted her hands on her hips and glared at Stone, sensing a certain amount of humor in his tone. "That's not funny."

"It's not funny for him either," he reminded her. "He's trying to keep you safe."

She frowned at that. "Fine, he gets points for that, but, wow, he needs to chill when he's talking to me."

"Yeah, that should be fun … to watch," Stone muttered.

"I didn't expect him to be quite so difficult."

"Terk has been to hell and back since his team was attacked. He knows this crap and has absolutely no problem with using force when it's needed," Stone explained calmly. "The problem is when people try to stop him or to interfere in what he considers the job he needs to do. You have to just let him do his job."

"And, in this case, he needed to blow that truck to smithereens?"

"Yes. I heard the argument with the other two about it, and he won. Believe me. You don't want to cross Terk when he thinks he's on the right side of things, and he usually is."

"Just because he *thinks* he's on the right side doesn't mean he *is*," she said irritably.

"Yeah, well, you'll have to be the one to tell him that." Stone smiled. "I don't think he's too worried about listening to the rest of us."

She groaned at that. "And I can't complain either, since he's trying to keep me safe. Well, the babies."

"In his mind, it's the same thing," Stone said gently. "Don't forget that."

"He doesn't even know me," she said, with a headshake. "It's not me he's trying to save."

"Of course it is. You're carrying the babies."

"Exactly, so it's not me. It's the babies."

"It's one and the same," he said, "and you're just being

difficult if you try to separate them from you."

Her jaw dropped, and she looked at him. "Oh my God, are you all like that?"

"If you mean, calling a spade a spade, then yes," he said, looking confused. "Why wouldn't I be?"

She raised her palms. "I don't know. Maybe because some niceties in life make it easier for all of us to get along."

"Nope." He shook his head. "Not in this case. That'll just make shit happen that we don't have time for, and we don't need drama. So, pick whatever side you want to be on and just make sure that you stay there. The rest of us will get back to the job at hand."

And, with that, he returned to his monitors and made her feel like she'd completely been neglecting her duties. She studied the monitors in front of her, but she couldn't see anything. "Should I be watching other monitors now that they're gone?"

"Nope, you need to keep watching those."

"Why?" She hated it, but all she could think was that he was trying to give her easy work.

"Because we want to see if anybody comes back, looking for these guys. And to see what happened to the vehicle."

"Oh," she said, once again feeling like an idiot. "Gosh, it's really taking me time to get the hang of this. I'm sorry."

"No need to be sorry," he muttered, his gaze obviously on the monitors in front of him. "It's just a fact of life that we all deal with here."

"Yeah, it's nothing at all like my world."

"And yet your world has somehow collided with his, so the two of you need to find a middle ground."

She sighed. "That's a little hard to do."

"No, it's not, not at all," Stone argued. "You both have

to decide what's important, and then you work toward it."

She looked over at him. "It sounds like you've either been to counseling or you're a therapist."

"No, not me," he snickered. "It goes back to calling a spade a spade and to not causing drama."

"Is there ever a place for drama?"

"Yes, … in the theater." When she burst out laughing, he turned and grinned at her.

"Maybe it's the babies," she admitted, "but, to be honest, I think it's just this whole situation. I don't know how to handle it, and I feel like a fish out of water."

"And nobody is expecting you to feel anything other than that. This is all about making it safe for both you and your babies … and everybody else for that matter. You can figure out your shit afterward."

"I hope so," she murmured, "because some of this is pretty complicated."

"No, it really isn't. You just need time to figure it out together."

"I don't know about that. We're complete strangers."

"No, I don't buy that," Stone murmured. "I can't imagine two energy workers, like you guys, not knowing each other."

"I don't know him," she repeated, looking over at Stone. "Is that why people think I'm lying?" The thought filled her with horror.

He looked at her. "No, I don't mean like that, but how is it that your energy doesn't know he's out there?"

"Oh," she said, looking at him, her eyebrows furrowed. "I don't know about my energy, about what it did or didn't know, but me, as a person, didn't know. And now that I do know, it doesn't make it any easier that Terk does the same shit I do. Or some of the same shit I do, I guess." She felt herself getting even more confused. "You guys are making me nuts."

Stone chuckled. "See? I don't think that'll wash either. The fact of the matter is that you and Terk have a situation you need to solve. So you need time to solve it. Preferably away from all these prying eyes."

"That'd be great"—she sighed—"but all we really have to do is figure out how we'll handle life after the babies are born."

"Which is another reason," he said calmly, "why you need to spend time together."

She shrugged. "I'm not sure what that'll do, since we'd likely just argue about parenting styles the whole time."

"Arguing isn't necessarily a problem, if it's productive."

"Is there such a thing as productive arguing?"

"Absolutely," he said, with a wicked note to his voice. "And you can tell me until you're blue in the face that you're not attracted to him, but I'd call you a liar as soon as you say it. So, I'll say it again. You need to spend time together and work this out."

"Attracted to him?" Her face flushed with color. "You remember that part I said about not knowing him?"

"Yeah, remember that part about you carrying his children?"

The heat washed over her face. "Sounds really bad when you say it like that."

"It's not really bad. It's a bizarre situation and one that we never could have imagined coming up. But here it is, and now you're in a situation that needs resolving. The best thing you can do is figure out if you guys have a relationship that's worth working on. But, either way, these babies will need both a mother and a father. You'll have to get along somehow, so why not try for something even better?"

"Good God," she whispered, as she sank back into her chair, really absorbing what he was saying. "You're really suggesting that we have to have a *real* relationship, aren't you?"

"Well, you'll have one either way," he said, looking at her. "I hope you're not planning on trying to keep him away from his kids. He's as much of a victim in this as you are. Besides, being the superprotective type that he is, he'd go ballistic."

"No, I wasn't planning on doing that." She felt sidelined by his other suggestion, yet ... was she really? Sure, she didn't know Terk, but she knew all the important things about him. Plus, she *was* attracted to him. Stone was right about that; she'd just didn't have time yet to sort through her feelings. She'd been a little busy. "I wasn't really thinking that we would be having a relationship."

"That's up to you." Stone turned toward her. "Just don't try to hide something like that because Terk will know."

"Of course he will," she muttered. "I wouldn't do that anyway."

"You know that he's attracted to you, right? I can also see that you're equally attracted to him. Anything less than that is being deceptive." Stone stood and stretched, then looked at the monitor again. "It looks like everybody is moving back toward home."

"Has everything been taken care of?"

"Yes, and we have a ton of prisoners coming back in."

"Did they leave them alive?"

"For now, but remember this attack group keeps knocking off their own guys. And everybody here is about out of patience, so anybody who crosses them won't survive. Either way, you need to be prepared to deal with that."

"I don't have a problem with it," she muttered. "I'm totally okay if none of these assholes survive. They were coming for me and my children, and, after what they've done, I really don't have any sympathy. Don't you have a place to just bury them out back?"

"We do," Stone confirmed cheerfully. "As of now. It's called the cemetery."

TERK UNDERSTOOD THE logic behind sorting out the truck mess, but he just didn't want anything to do with it. As he marched his prisoner toward the compound, he heard Stone saying that Terk's partners in crime from England had just landed. "Just in time," he muttered, rubbing his forehead.

"You could let me go," Camo Guy said.

"That ain't happening. Besides, you'd be lucky if you got one mile away."

"What are you talking about?"

"Everybody else who's worked on this shit job," he muttered, "has been shot the minute they met failure."

"I didn't fail."

"Well, unless getting captured was part of your cover," Terk said, "you failed."

"Maybe it was," he said, with a smirk.

"Like you have any clue what's going on."

"I have a good idea," the prisoner said, shaking his head. "I'm not sure you do though."

"Oh, I know what's going on," Terk replied.

"I doubt it. I've been at this from the beginning," the

prisoner said. "And, man, what a process. You know, if you hadn't been such a cagey bastard, they might have left you alive."

"They might have, *huh*? What was I supposed to tell them to stop them from killing me and my team?"

"They wanted to know what your plans were."

"Well, I didn't have any plans, but they would have had a better chance of finding out by picking up the damn phone."

"Bullshit. Everybody who loses their job has plans. They didn't want you setting up a department or your own private company."

Of course Terk had already considered that scenario, which had merit. "Maybe, but they didn't have to try to kill the entire team."

"The weapon needed testing anyway, but unfortunately that failed." He laughed. "And believe me. They've been trying to boost and improve it ever since."

"I'm sure they have," he muttered. "That's what was in the truck."

"Sure, but what makes you think it's the only one?"

"If it isn't, we'll find the others," Terk said, with a snort. "Don't you worry."

"Oh, I'm not worried, but you should be."

"Yeah, so you're on scaring duty or what?" Terk asked in a caustic tone. Once they got back to the compound, the prisoner was put into the other jail cell, alongside Jerome. He looked over at that guy and asked, "Who's this?"

"One of your cronies," Terk replied.

"I hate to tell you, but he isn't. I don't know this guy at all."

"Yeah, well, you also work for a guy who doesn't let the

left hand know what the right hand is doing," Terk snapped. "So, yeah, he's part of the same locally hired lackeys."

The two men looked at each other, like they were complete strangers, and, from the first impression Terk got, they probably were. If so, that would make his job even harder. But his second impression was that these guys were acting and did know each other. Terk looked over at Logan. "Is somebody standing guard?"

"Yeah," Logan said. "I can take the first shift."

Terk nodded, pulling him away ever-so-slightly, and asked in a low tone, "Do we have any recording devices set up?"

"Yes, absolutely. Plus, I'll be around."

"Stay out of their way, but get video and audio," Terk suggested. "And I won't be very far away."

Logan nodded. "I've got this."

"No, sorry, that's not my point. I think something else is going on." And, with that, he wouldn't say any more. But, with a final look at the two prisoners, who just stared at him blankly, Terk nodded. "Have fun, guys."

And he turned and walked away. Instead of going into the kitchen, which is where he wanted to go, Terk headed straight up to the control room and gave the password. It opened immediately, and Stone stood there, grinning.

"There you are. She's worried," Stone stepped back to reveal Celia, curled up in a chair, chewing on her fingernail.

Relief washed over Terk. She was safe. And too damn adorable. "Come on," he said, holding out his hand. "We need to talk."

She turned her gaze to him. "Nice greeting. How about something more like, *Hey, nice to see you. Glad all is well, and you're safe. If you don't mind, can we talk for a few minutes?*"

"Stop." He glared at her. "I really don't need that shit right now." And, with that, he grabbed her hand and hauled her out. She protested the whole way, but he didn't give a crap. His emotions were all over the place. That was unusual in itself but his lack of a sense of control? That was something else. When he got to his room, he opened the door, popped her in, and followed, closing the door behind him.

Looking around, Celia noted where they were, and she crossed her arms over her chest. "What do you want? Don't you know what manners are?"

"Listen. I'm tired. I'm fed up. The rest of my team will be here within the hour, and we have a few things to sort out."

She glared at him. "Like what?"

"Like this." And he pulled her into his arms and kissed her. The depth of his passion hit her—and him—as soon as their lips touched, like some energy vortex inside him just loosened into this pounding tempo. He had never experienced anything like it. Plus, her response slid through him at the same time. He presumed her senses had been wide open for that to even occur, and, when he lifted his head, he noted a dazed expression on her face.

"What the hell was that?" she whispered.

"I don't know, but I sure as hell want to find out." And this time, when he lowered his head, he tried to be gentler. He tried to coax a response instead of storming in, but it was the same explosive kiss as last time.

So much energy fired between them that it was like being sucked into a wind tunnel—tremulous, stormy, yet addictive. When he finally broke away again, he stepped back, his hands shaking, as he stared down at them. He looked over to see the same look of complete shock on her face.

"Good God. Is that us?"

He nodded ever-so-slowly. "I think so."

"You *think* so?"

"You tell me then." Terk shrugged. "I've never felt anything like this before."

"Neither have I." Her words tumbled out of her mouth in a rush. "I never thought such a thing was even possible."

"No?" he asked, as confused as she was. He walked over to the end of the bed and sat down. He didn't even know what to think. From wanting desperately to pull her into his arms, to ensure she was safe, and back to the kiss that he had never intended to impose on her. However, the reaction he had never thought was even possible was evidence that he had done the right thing for both of them. "I don't even know what just happened," he muttered, looking over at her, "but it says a lot about where we're at."

"No," she said, as she sat down beside him. "It says a lot about where we're at when we're together. Potent."

"Meaning that, if we're apart, it'll be easier?" he asked, with a note of humor.

She gave him a wry smile. "I guess that's naïve of me."

"Yep, it sure is. I get that you're hoping that maybe it'll go away."

"I wouldn't say that. I'm not hoping that it goes away," she corrected. "I mean, at the moment, all I can think about right now is that kiss."

"Yeah, me too." He stared at her hungrily.

"You brought me up here ..." And then she stopped and raised her hand. "Let me rephrase that. You dragged me up here to talk to me about something—"

"Yeah," he interrupted. "*That.*"

"What do you mean, *that?*" she cried out in shock. "You mean the kiss?"

"Well, I've been wanting to do that for quite a while," he murmured.

She stared at him. "You know that there are some customary niceties and a bit of a romantic approach, as opposed to just going pure caveman."

He stared at her for a moment, then he burst out laughing. "And you know what? ... It didn't even occur to me. The need was so damn strong, I just did what I thought was right for me—right for both of us, I think. Obviously it was seriously necessary. I've never felt anything like that before."

"So you keep telling me, but that doesn't explain what you wanted to discuss or settle or whatever."

"Nope, you're right, I was hoping we could discuss whatever we have going on for a relationship. Our future."

"We don't have a relationship, but it's obvious that a whole lot of energy is going on between us."

"You don't think that your kidnappers knew that, ... that we would have some energy bond when they did this, do you?"

She held her hand over her belly protectively.

He looked at her and then at her belly. "I have no idea because I don't know what the parameters were that even qualified you for this position."

She snorted at that. "I'm not sure there is such a thing, and you, sir, really need to work on how you talk to a woman. That didn't sound nice at all."

He groaned. "I'm tired. I'm so over this mess, and I just want to hold you and to kiss you until we're both blind again." He sighed. "All I'm trying to say is that I want to be in the lives of these babies, and I'd like to explore what we could have. I want a relationship that works for both of us."

"So far we don't have anything but temper and passion."

He gave her a lopsided smile. "Honestly, that's quite a bit more than a lot of people have."

CHAPTER 11

PRIVATELY CELIA AGREED with Terk, but she was still reeling from the onslaught of her emotions. "I don't know what the hell just happened, but you are deadly."

"No," he corrected gently, "we are deadly together, and that's what makes the difference."

She nodded. "I can get behind that, and, yes, I would like to see what we have when this is all over with. But I have to admit that I don't know what form that'll take."

He gave her a tiny smile. "You don't have any psychic intuition about that?"

"No." Her eyes went wide as she stared at him.

"I don't care about premonitions either, but I do get them sometimes," he said, as he gently caressed her extended abdomen. "And you can bet that the babies are listening in."

"Are they really?" She was fascinated in spite of herself. "I wonder what they're thinking?"

"Thinking, not so much. Feeling," he noted. "There's a strong bond already among all of us."

"I know," she said, smiling wistfully. "That much I can feel. I just didn't have a clue if you felt it too."

"Oh, yes," he murmured, "I definitely feel it. And that's another reason we need to sort this out as soon as we can."

"So, what are your plans? I don't know what to do about my small apartment. The bills are being paid, but it's not

173

really big enough for the twins. Do you even have a place, or will we be staying here with Levi and Ice? I do feel like I've already overstayed my welcome."

"You're always welcome here," he said, with a firm smile. "They would never chase you out. I could find a place for us to go spend a few days."

"That ... might be helpful. Though I'm not certain it would be wise, given our energy," she said. "Yet it's still better than most of the ideas you've had so far."

He raised his eyebrows and gave her a taunting smile. "What's the matter? You scared?"

"Terrified," she admitted bluntly.

He burst out laughing. "Okay, at least that's honest."

"I don't know what's going on here." She sighed. "And everything is happening so fast that I just need a bit of time."

"Time you can have, at least until we get to the bottom of this. And then you and I will go off and spend a few days together."

"And where is it you're thinking we'll go? I don't really have any place here."

"I know a place. It's on a lake. It would give us some privacy to spend a few days and talk."

"That would be nice."

And, with that, he said, "You're looking tired, so maybe you should lie down and try to get a nap." After getting her settled on the bed, he disappeared quickly.

She stared around the room in amazement because it was his room. He had just casually brought her in and told her to take a nap. Like that would happen. She couldn't forget the feel of his lips on hers and the instant energy kindled that they were both keeping banked.

Whenever they let it loose, *if* they did let it loose, it

would likely burn them to ashes. She tried to remind herself that it was supposedly a choice, though it seemed inevitable. Part of her couldn't wait, and another part of her was terrified of whatever this was she was starting with this man she barely knew.

All her relationships, up until now, had been with men who she knew she could handle, but Terk was in a class all his own. Not only was he a powerful psychic but he was a very capable military man. And all her prior relationships paled in comparison to him, something she needed to remember. The other men she had known were all amiable, easy to get along with, and essentially boring.

Whereas Terk ignited her senses, heightening her responses, stoking every fire within her. Good or bad, for the first time, he made her feel alive in ways she didn't even know were possible.

And that kiss …

Well, hell, it'd be a long cold day before she could ever forget the sensation of being in his arms, totally possessed. And that's exactly what it was, it was all of her possessed by him, 100 percent. And a part of her couldn't wait for it to happen again.

TERK STOOD IN the hallway a few moments, taking time to get his body and heart back in check. He wasn't exactly sure what the hell would happen, but he'd always known in his heart of hearts that, when he met somebody who was right, it would happen fast.

And apparently Celia was the right person. Then he'd known that when he met her. But, for the first time, all his senses aligned to the same acknowledgment.

Celia was the right person for him.

She wasn't sure about any of this, but he could hardly blame her. She'd been to hell and back, and he hadn't exactly been much help.

Not going to be much help for a while yet.

He knew that because he was still dealing with getting to the bottom of all this, so they could move forward with their lives. Whatever that would bring. What he knew for sure was that he would never miss the opportunity to create a relationship with his twins.

Grinning to himself, he quickly shifted mentally and headed down toward the prisoners. As he walked in, Logan stood, smiled at him. "Not a peep out of them so far."

He nodded. "Wasn't really expecting there to be one." He looked over at the one prisoner that he'd marched in first. "Ready to talk, Jerome?"

"Hell no," he snorted. "You've got way too much of that woo-woo shit happening here."

"That's why I came down to talk to you," Terk admitted, grinning, "to see what else I can get from you."

At that, a name popped into Jerome's mind.

"Wow, who the hell is Boyd?"

Jerome froze and stared at him. "No, no, no. Now that is not human. None of that stuff. That right there is a damn good reason for them to take you out," he said, pointing one finger at Terk. "You don't get to just jump into my head and get all this shit." He looked terrified and was unraveling by the second. "And they won't believe me when I tell them that I didn't give it to you."

"Nope, they won't. It is comical, isn't it? I mean, you might as well just give up the ghost because they'll blame you anyway."

"But I didn't do shit," he roared. "You're the one who needs to be put down, like the dog you are."

"What the hell's going on here?" the second prisoner asked.

"Shut the fuck up," the first one snarled, as he sat back down.

"Hey, shut it," the newest prisoner snarled. "I don't know what the hell you've got to do with any of this, but you don't talk to me like that."

Jerome shot him a look but subsided.

Terk smiled at Camo Guy. "You know that I'll get all the information I want out of your loose-lipped friend there beside you."

Camo Guy glared at him. "Don't know what the hell you're doing, but it's just plain wrong."

"I don't care if it's wrong or not." Terk grinned. "My method works, and, when I need information, ... I really don't give a shit if you like my methods or not."

Camo Guy glared at Terk, then suddenly moved forward, and completely shocked everyone here, reaching for Jerome through the bars, grabbing him by the head, swinging him around. An audible *crack* was heard, as his neck snapped. They couldn't react in time to stop it. "Now what the hell will you ask him?" he asked, with a sneer.

"Well, you must be Bill."

That had Camo Guy freezing in his tracks.

Terk continued. "And you just answered some other questions I had," Terk replied, trying hard to bring his own fury under control. "First, you're an asshole. Second, obviously you're connected, so now we have a link confirmed."

"You don't know shit," he snapped, as he settled back into his seat, "but you're not getting anything out of me."

"I already got lots out of you, and believe me. Your bosses will be very interested in hearing it." Terk knew that this guy was pretty rattled right now, and all Terk could do was hold in his anger and wait for Jerome to be removed from his cell. The chances of his being alive at this point were pretty nonexistent.

Terk knew Logan had sent out an alarm, and soon footsteps ran toward them. Merk checked on the prisoners, then glared over at Logan. "That wasn't exactly what we thought would happen."

"Hell no, he grabbed him through the bars."

"It's almost as if he's got some practice."

Bill just sat back, his eyes closed.

When Levi showed up, he stared at the prisoners in shock. "What the hell happened?"

"Yeah," Terk said, pointing. "Bill reached through bars, grabbed Jerome, and broke his neck. Not even a conscious thought about doing anything other than what he had planned to do. It was deliberate. But then I had been saying that I would get all I needed for information off Jerome. Apparently Jerome knew something that Bill was afraid I'd get," he said, staring at the remaining prisoner.

"You murdered your own teammate?" Logan stared at him, with disgust. "What kind of guys are you?"

"Loyal."

"Loyal to the money, you mean."

"No. You don't know anything about it. You don't know who you're dealing with. If you want to stay alive through all this, you need to follow orders. Besides, we're already sanctioned for this. So, do your worst."

At his use of the term *sanctioned*, Terk felt his blood thinning. He glanced over at Levi and saw the same recognition on his face. The terminology was important, but he didn't want Bill to know that he'd let slip something major. Terk turned to Levi. "I'll run upstairs for a minute."

"Yeah, sure." Levi nodded. "I'll bring down a couple more men. We'll put Jerome in the cooler."

"That's great," Terk replied. "When does the body count start to become a problem?"

"It was a problem a while ago, but we're dealing with it."

Terk raced upstairs to Ice's office. And there he asked, "Has my team come in yet?"

"They're en route. Problems?"

He quickly told her what the newest prisoner had said.

"*Sanctioned*," she repeated and whistled. "Do you really think it's a government contract to take you out?"

He frowned. "I don't know, but I'm willing to look at any and all options to find out. It's always been a real option."

She shook her head at that. "We're already getting hit ourselves. We have way too many bodies right now."

"And you've got another one." Terk then explained what Bill had just done. She stared at Terk, shocked, her jaw dropping. "He just broke his neck like that? One of his own team?"

"Afraid that I might get information from Jerome, using my wonderfully nefarious ways," he said, with an eye roll.

"You probably could have."

"Possibly," he agreed, "but I felt like I'd already gotten everything that I could get. But I don't know about this Bill guy." Terk hesitated, and then added, "I was wondering about bringing down Celia. But, if my team is coming, that might be all I need."

"They should be here soon. You've got four coming."

"Yeah, I'd initially told them all to stay back, but that wasn't happening. As it turns out, it's good they came, but we needed to leave some in England to look after everyone back home."

"Good enough. I've got rooms ready for them." Just then the phone rang. She glanced at it and winced. "*Great,* CIA," she muttered. "They've been on my case an awful lot more than I would like."

"Anything I can do to help?"

"God no, your name is mud with the CIA," she said cheerfully. "And DGSE for that matter. MI6 is constantly checking in with us too. It seems that everybody wants to know where you are."

"Well, you can tell them that I'm here and that they won't get rid of me that easily."

"Really? What is it you're thinking of?" she asked, looking over at him.

"Well, I have to relocate somewhere, and honestly MI6 has been okay to work with."

"Setting up your own business?" she asked.

Terk nodded. "One to start but this compound is not big enough for all of us."

"No, it sure isn't," she said, laughing. "Start your own then. We are all happy to see where it goes."

"At least the guys are planning on my doing something along that line."

"It would be good." She grinned. "We have Bullard in Africa, and, if you were in England"—she rubbed her hands together—"that would be a huge help."

"Don't get too optimistic about it just yet," Terk said, a

warning in his tone. "We're a long way away from being set up yet."

"No, of course not," she agreed in perfect innocence, but her eyes were gleaming.

He groaned. "I knew I shouldn't have said anything."

"You absolutely should have. Are you kidding? What about Charles?"

"He's probably the first one who suggested it to me. I'd already been thinking about it but hadn't gotten that far."

"Yeah, Charles could use a hand over there," she murmured. "He hates to admit that the years are piling up on him."

"Hates to admit? It's crap, and you know it. That guy just won't quit."

"And I want to be just like him when I grow up," she announced.

He chuckled. "You and me both. In the meantime, we have a problem here to deal with."

"Yep," she said, "and I need to call the CIA back."

He nodded and stepped away. "You do that. If they want a meeting, set it up here."

"Oh, now that's an interesting thought."

"At least make it close enough that I could potentially get some information."

"Wouldn't that be lovely," she said, with a smile. "Let me talk to this guy and see what I can do."

With that, Terk had to be content. He turned and walked out, leaving her to deal with her business, even while his mind was consumed with his own. And just as he walked toward the kitchen, he heard vehicles arrive and looked out to see his men.

He walked out the side door, a big grin on his face, as

Damon, Gage, Calum, and Wade stepped from the truck. They exchanged greetings, as he looked at them all. "Is everybody okay back at the base?"

"Yeah, they definitely are," Damon said. "And we've set up security, which our two very lovely sisters appear to monitor on an energy level for any problem."

"What about Tasha?" he asked, looking at Damon.

"Yeah, she's grumpy, but she's on it. I honestly think we did a hell of a job when we enlarged that team."

"I agree," Terk murmured, "though not everybody has the same abilities. However, there are lots of ways to contribute."

"Noted," Damon replied, "but it won't be long before even those who didn't think they had abilities, start developing a few."

"Particularly with the bonds between you all, we'll be seeing a lot more of it soon." Terk nodded.

"So what's going on here?" Calum asked.

"The shit has been hitting the fan constantly." Then he brought them all up to date.

"What about Celia?" Damon asked, looking at Terk in concern.

"Yeah, that's one of those unresolved issues at the moment," he said, "and I'm not exactly sure where it's going."

"No?" Wade looked at him, with the hint of a grin. "Yet apparently you're interested."

Terk winced. "And that's the problem with psychics. You guys are always picking up information that isn't necessarily intended for you or needed to be passed around."

"I don't think it makes a damn bit of difference when it comes to you anyway," Wade said immediately. "If you wanted to block us, you would."

"Can't be bothered." Then Terk nodded. "You're right. I am interested. She is too, but we have some ugly history that had nothing to do with either one of us, so we'll need to get through that first."

"Got it." Damon then asked, "Is she really a scientist who has been studying energy and psychic phenomena?"

Terk nodded. "Doesn't that just beat all? And clearly somebody then decided the work was important enough to pick up and run with."

"It is an interesting idea."

At that, Wade stepped forward. "So, the truck that you blew up? I want to see it."

Terk shrugged. "Sure, but any particular reason?"

"The whole way over, I was studying what might take us all down like that, and I was trying to figure out whether this was an EMP and if that would even do the job."

"I imagine it would," Terk noted. "And if we saw anybody else around us who had the same reaction at the same time, then it's quite possible that they have abilities that we didn't know about—and even potentially *they* didn't know about."

"Right," he said, with a clipped nod. "We need to see it."

At the same time, Logan turned up, and they all greeted each other. Terk knew this would be an ongoing thing until everybody had met his team.

Logan asked, "Did I hear you say you wanted to see the truck? I can take you down. How many?"

"Just two," Wade replied. "We need to get everybody settled in."

On that note they split, with the three men heading toward the truck that they suspected held the remains of a weapon that had yet to be retrieved.

As Terk walked inside with Damon and Calum, heading toward the kitchen, Terk found Alfred sitting here, a big smile on his face. "You've got four more mouths to feed," Terk noted. "Hope you're up for it."

"More than up for it," Alfred said comfortably. "A house should ring with laughter," he murmured. "And, if it doesn't, it needs to be a damn war room."

"Well, we've got the war room covered," Terk replied.

Just then Ice walked in. "In a big way," she said, looking over at Alfred. "I don't want you to bring out the good silverware or anything, but we have an in-house meeting tomorrow morning at 0900, with the CIA."

Alfred looked at her in surprise. "In that case," he said caustically, "I'll hide the good silverware." And he quickly walked to the dining room.

CHAPTER 12

CELIA HEARD *CIA*, and her spirit collapsed. She stepped into the kitchen to stare at Ice. "Are we thinking there's a problem with the CIA?"

"They think there's a problem with us," Ice said, with a calm smile. "We do have an accumulation of dead bodies that need to be dealt with and hushed up."

"Right." Celia winced. "Not exactly my skill set."

Ice chuckled. "Unless you're in the business, like I am, it's not part of anybody's skill set. But we've dealt with the CIA before, so why not here?" she asked.

"Does that unnerve you?" Terk asked, turning to look at Celia.

"Yes." She took a deep breath. "I guess everything unnerves me at the moment," she said, with a wave of her hand. "So it's probably not a fair assessment right now."

"It's been a pretty crazy day." Ice looked over at her. "Do you need something to eat?"

"I could eat." She laughed, patting her tummy. "Junior is getting pretty busy."

"*Juniors*," Terk corrected.

She nodded. "I'm still struggling to even identify with the theory of an actual child, and yet there are two, so I find it just makes it easier for me to think in terms of it being one, instead of the craziness that's about to come with twins."

Ice just laughed out loud. "It is crazy change, but, if you have people around you who can help, it makes a huge difference."

"I don't know what I'll have."

"Family?"

She shook her head, "No, I was raised in the foster care system. I don't have any family that I know of."

"Oh, and that's an interesting thing too," Ice noted. "I wonder if we should do a search and see if we could find any?"

Celia stared at her in surprise. "Is that something you can find out?"

Ice nodded. "If there's information to be found, I can find it."

"I always assumed all those records were sealed."

"In adoptions, they are sealed in some cases, until the child becomes an adult," Ice explained. "Different states have different laws regarding foster care records and such, so it's all over the map. I can see if there's some information in your history somewhere that would give us a clue. And, of course, we have DNA searches we can do now as well. If you want me to, that is."

"That would be great, thanks. I'm not expecting any-thing though, since I was told I had no family."

"But people tell lies all the time." Ice quickly jotted a note to herself about it. "Look. Our delayed dinner will be here in a bit, but let's see if we can get you something to fuel up on in the meantime. Alfred is working on putting out a spread for us."

At that, Celia gasped. "Oh, gosh, I should be helping him," She bolted into the kitchen, apologizing profusely.

Alfred just patted her gently on the shoulder. "Don't you worry about it. I have things under control."

"I know. I know you do, but I said that I'd help."

"And you can." He pointed to a big mixer. "We're doing mashed potatoes."

"In that?" she gasped.

"Did you see how many potatoes were involved?"

She peered down and shook her head. "I wouldn't even guess how much you need to cook to make any of this happen."

"That's just fine," Alfred replied, "because it's not your job."

She set the mixer going and kept adding salt and butter until she thought it was good; then she had Alfred come over and take a look. He slipped in his pinkie finger and tasted it. "Not bad but I think I'd prefer to add a bit of whipping cream."

And, with that note, he tossed in what looked like cups and cups of whipping cream, combining it well, and then added fresh green onions that he'd chopped up. "It's all yours, my dear."

The aroma was heavenly. By the time she pulled up the head of the mixer and scooped the potatoes into a serving bowl, she was starving. "This is beautiful," she mumbled. "I didn't realize how hungry I am."

"And that's good. Babies need lots in order to grow properly."

"These babies need a whole lot less than what they tell me they need." She chuckled.

Alfred had Terk set the table, and very quickly everybody else started gathering, as if the smell had worked its way throughout the entire compound. Celia wouldn't be at all surprised if it had. Some serious eaters were here before, and now they had four more from Terk's team.

She walked into the dining room and immediately felt pinned down by laser beams that came out of nowhere. She froze, feeling like a deer in the headlights, and looked at Terk. He just got up, walked around the table, and introduced her to his team. She could barely even nod, as she stared at the men. Their energy reached her like a wall of suspicion. "Good God."

One of them raised an eyebrow. "What's up?"

"All of you, ... your energy is one thing. ... Then you look all badass and dangerous," she said, almost afraid to continue. "How in the hell did you guys even get partners? Women should run away in terror."

"They're not scared of us," one of the guys replied.

"Well, that had to have been some trick," she muttered. She studied the team, trying to keep her own senses down, but these guys were on serious overload. The energy around them was popping. "You guys don't notice it?" she asked, looking over at Levi and Ice.

"If you mean the electricity in the air, yeah, we notice that," she said, "but it's never been anything we were capable of accessing, so it's not something we worry about."

At that, Terk looked over at Celia. "And what do you see?"

"Energy. ... I mean, an incredible amount of energy among all of you."

The first man who'd spoken nodded. "It's the work we do," he noted gently.

"So I understand. I do too, but I did it alone or with people who didn't have very strong skill sets."

"And that's the problem," Terk said. "As you had mentioned, when you hook up with other people who have similar … skills, … particularly those that we have, you learn and you learn quickly, and we do generate more and more energy."

"Well, I guess that's waiting for me then," she muttered, hoping it was true.

"It does get easier," Terk said calmly. "You'll be surprised at how quickly you become comfortable with it all."

"Maybe." She studied Terk closely. "But the thing is, the energy is swirling around all of you. Not only are you tired but you're utilizing energy to keep yourself functioning until you can crash."

"We've been traveling for a while." Damon nodded. "And we're okay to get up and to go to work, if we need to, but, yes, … rest would be helpful. But along with that comes food."

And she watched them as they served themselves huge amounts of food, loading their plates more than full. She stared at this in wonder; then she raised her gaze and caught sight of Terk, smirking. "I have a lot to learn, don't I?"

"That you do," he agreed, "but one of the best sources of energy is food, so eat up."

"Ah, okay, but so is everything else around us. Thankfully energy is limitless—the plants outside, the ground underneath our feet. There are a lot of ways to source energy."

"There is, but this kind of energy that goes from zero to 100 percent in less than five seconds requires a medium to tap into, when we're drained and we need more. Then we can pull from Mother Earth as well," Terk explained calmly.

Celia sat and thought about that. "That's an area that I haven't had very much to do with. It's not as if I need energy constantly."

"No, but, when you get tired during the day, what do you do?" Terk asked.

She thought about it. "I just open my senses, then rest and recharge, I guess."

"Right." Terk nodded. "However, in our line of work, we can't open our senses like that, in case somebody else is out there who can do what we do."

She sat back in her chair, understanding immediately. "See? I hadn't even considered that."

"Because it's not the field that you're in," someone she thought was Damon pointed out. "So, we're always protective and mindful of our energy. It's unusual for us to have a place like this here, with Ice and Levi, where we're safe and not under an onslaught of attacks."

"Well, you will be, particularly if you stay here long enough," Ice said, grinning in such a nonchalant way that Levi burst out laughing.

"It's not how we intend to let guests get comfortable," Levi noted. "You do know that, right?"

Celia grinned at him. "I think you guys are in your element, honestly." She shook her head. "I've never seen anybody quite so happy to be checking their weapons and figuring out where the bad guys are. I mean, Stone is happy as a clam and completely in his element up in that little room. And, for such a big guy, ... couldn't you have made the control room like twice the size?"

"We weren't necessarily thinking of Stone running it at the time." Ice chuckled. "Yet, considering that he's taken to it, like a duck to water, I won't exactly pull it away from him now."

"No, that makes sense. I couldn't imagine that you'd

planned that room that way."

"It was part of the original building that we converted to the control room."

Just then Stone walked in. "Did I hear my name?"

"Yep," Celia nodded. "They're talking about taking you out of the control room and giving you a different job on the compound."

The look on his face was absolutely priceless.

When Levi started snickering, Stone looked at him, then to Celia and back again. "You better be joking."

Levi couldn't contain it anymore and started to laugh out loud.

Ice nodded. "Oh, toughen up, Stone. She's just putting you on."

He looked over at Celia in horror. "Why would you even joke about such a thing?" he cried out. "That's my place. You saw it. I belong there."

She grinned at him. "I know that, and, if you'd walked in a few seconds earlier, you would have heard me angling to have that room made bigger for you."

He glared at her suspiciously. "What? Now you're calling me fat?"

"No, I wouldn't say that, but, now that you mentioned it, you're definitely not tiny. Although, in fairness, it is emphasized in that small room."

He looked at the dinner spread out in front of him and patted his tummy. "Well, no way I'm getting smaller anytime soon. Not with all this wonderful food here. I've had plenty of days where the food was barely edible."

"Yeah, were you on cooking duty?" Celia came back immediately.

He glared at her. "How come you're being so mean all of

a sudden?"

She burst out laughing. "Because you're so easy to tease."

"I am not. You know that," he said, coming in with a ferocious growl.

But she grinned at him impudently. "Oh, yes, you are. See? I've heard that growl for what it is now, and it doesn't scare me anymore."

Stone looked over at Terk. "You're taking her away with you. Aren't you?"

"I am," Terk said, amusement lighting his face. "And it sounds like she will fit in perfectly."

"She would at that." Stone nodded. "Good choice."

Terk snorted at that. "Not sure I had anything to do with the choice, but now that she's here and doing so well …"

She listened to the conversation going on around her, a little worried that she wasn't supposed to know what this was all about and, at the same time, worried that she did know because it was a conversation she didn't want to get into. She glared at them. "Enough of that talk."

"Oh no, no way." Stone shook his head. "What's good for the goose is good for the gander. You're teasing me. I'll be teasing you."

"Fine," she snapped. "I'll leave you alone then."

He burst out laughing. "Nope, that won't save your sorry ass either."

She shoved him a huge bowl of potatoes. "Maybe this will help."

He accepted it gladly. "Oh, I do love my mashed potatoes."

As he served himself a huge helping, she shook her head. "So you guys work all the time, but how else do you manage to not gain weight here?" She spoke with a touch of envy in her voice.

"We all work out," Ice said. "Staying fit is part of our physical requirements too, so we're always ready for whatever life throws our way."

"Well, I sure as hell wasn't ready for that attack," she said, "so maybe I should be taking pointers."

"Most people don't have to deal with the stuff that we deal with," Ice said gently. "So I can't imagine many would be prepared. Besides, this crazy situation would never happen again or in the same way, so prepping would be pretty hard to do."

Celia groaned. "Meaning, just carry on with my same old ways and hopefully I won't get into trouble again?"

"Something like that," Ice said, with a rogue smile. "More than that, I don't think these guys will let you get into trouble anymore."

Celia looked around at the table, but everybody was focused on their food and not necessarily looking at her. "I hope not." Still, she felt a little uncomfortable. She didn't know the rest of Levi's team or Terk's team, who had just arrived. To her, they were all strangers, and that made her feel like an oddity. She looked over at Terk. "Have you worked with these guys for long?"

He nodded. "Years, and, yes, they're all safe. They have all been vetted many times over."

"By whom?" she asked curiously.

He lifted his head and looked at her briefly, then flashed her a bright smile. "Me." And, with that, he went back to eating.

She had to wonder what that meant but figured it had something to do with energy work, reminding her that there was so much more that she could learn from Terk and his team. She would have to get him into the lab with her, one way or another.

"Don't even think about it," Terk declared, glaring at her.

She glared right back. "Why not?"

"Hey now, you two. Include everybody else in the conversation," Levi said. "You're at my table, so don't get rude on me." He pointed his fork at Terk. "You know the rules."

Terk nodded. "Sorry." He looked over at her. "When we have a conversation here, it's for everybody."

"Fine," she said, "so why won't you come to the lab?" At the word *lab*, every member of Terk's team immediately straightened and focused on the conversation, no longer interested in their food.

"I won't be one of your guinea pigs," Terk said, and all of his men immediately shook their heads.

"Oh, hell no," Wade snapped.

"No guinea pigs here. Not happening." Damon's rejection was the loudest.

She glared at Terk. "How am I ever going to know what the hell you guys do and how you do it? If I don't study it, I cannot understand it."

"Who said you would study anything?" Gage asked.

"I'm a scientist," she announced. "It's what I do."

"Maybe it's what you *did*." He gave her such a hard glance that there was no mistaking his attitude. "Not one of us would take kindly to being tested, like a lab rat."

Her shoulders sagged as she sat back and frowned at them all. "Are you all going to be this difficult?"

Immediately all five of them nodded, and she didn't need to read their minds; she could read their faces.

No testing.

Not happening.

Never, never, never.

She looked over at Ice. "I guess you don't have any pull on this one, do you?"

Ice immediately shook her head. "Nope, and honestly, if it were me, I'd be on their side too."

Levi agreed. "Absolutely."

Stone grinned. "Same here."

"Why?" she asked, the scientist in her kicking in even more. "What is it about testing that makes you all so afraid?"

At the term *afraid*, they all glared at her.

She raised both hands. "It really is fear though," she said, trying to keep her voice calm, nonthreatening. "And I don't understand it. Help me to understand where you're coming from. I'm serious, please."

TERK LOOKED OVER at her. Celia really was serious, and she really didn't understand. "Because our whole world is about protection," he murmured. "We look after ourselves to keep ourselves safe. The minute anybody knows anything about us, it becomes a weapon they can use against us."

She slowly closed her mouth. "Is everything in your world about death and dying?"

"Pretty much." He nodded. "More about keeping those things off the table."

"Wow." She stared at him. "I'm not sure I can live like that."

"You'll adjust," Terk replied.

She glared at him. "Or maybe you'll adjust," she

snapped.

He just gave her the briefest of smiles. "One of us can see parts of the future."

"And *one* of us"—she glared at him—"is determined to make her own decisions."

At that, the others looked up, their gazes going from one to the other, but they now ate as they watched Terk and Celia, barely suppressing their smiles, looking at each other like they were thoroughly enjoying the entertainment.

CHAPTER 13

"F INE," CELIA MUTTERED, when Terk remained silent. *Back to something completely unrelated then.* "So, what's happening with the CIA?" At that, Levi and Ice got into a conversation over it all, and Celia listened with half an ear. It sounded like, regardless of her intentions on the matter, Terk would not let her slip away into the night and make her own plans for her life, and that was distressing.

Or was it? Something was also reassuring about his attitude.

She knew that she needed to stay safe, but surely they could get this all handled before she was even close to giving birth because the thought of this chaos continuing and destroying her life forever was too depressing to even contemplate.

By the time dinner was over, she felt the fatigue hit her again. She looked over, but the other men were talking, seemingly energized. So was her issue really one of fatigue, or was it maybe the stress of carrying twins?

Something else she had no experience with.

She got up to return her plate to the kitchen. Immediately Terk was beside her, and, as she turned around to see what else she could do to help, he shook his head. "Not tonight. Come on upstairs to bed."

"What if I don't want to go to bed?" she asked. Only,

when replaying her words, she knew it sounded like she was two years old. "Jesus, I must be more tired than I thought."

"You are. Come on. Let's get you up to bed."

"Why you though?"

"Well, those are my babies you're carrying," he noted humorously. "And everybody on my team, and Merk as well, all have partners now."

"What? So that makes us the odd ones out or something?"

Yep, he said in her mind. *But we're not odd ones out at all.*

She stopped and stared. *Really? We're the ones who made twins without even sleeping together. Remember?*

Terk laughed with delight at the joke, and she couldn't keep herself from giggling. *Oh God. Have they already stamped us as a couple?* she asked in horror.

It's what usually happens around here, he replied. *Just because we haven't got our relationship together doesn't mean that they don't have it all figured out for us.*

She groaned. *And I suppose the more we protest, the more they'll enjoy it, right?*

They've all been through it. They understand what a roller coaster ride it can be. He stooped down to look at her carefully, as he gently guided her to the elevator. *They know what we're going through, and, although they have sympathy, they won't let us off the hook either.*

Of course not. She sighed. *It is sad though.*

What is? he asked.

It just feels sad somehow, and I don't even know why.

Terk frowned. *Because you didn't have all the romance that you wanted?*

I don't even think the romance was part of it, but maybe more of that sense of being chosen for the right reasons, instead of being chosen because I was the optimal lab rat.

That lab rat thing is exactly what the guys were talking about earlier, Terk reminded her, *about how they felt about being your test subjects, about why they don't want to be a part of your research.*

The subject of testing aside, when it comes to pregnancy and other relationship issues, she murmured, *women want a little bit more.*

TERK KNEW ABOUT the whole relationship mess, as he'd watched off and on with Ice, Levi, Damon, Wade, Calum, Gage, and pretty much everyone else. He remembered how Ice had also wanted something similar. Out loud he said, "But I certainly understand that need to feel like this wasn't just an off-the-cuff moment that happened randomly, instead of you and I choosing to be together and both of us wholly involved in the fun way to create the twins."

"Exactly." She looked at him.

He shrugged. "I do get a lot of things in life, even though I don't spend too much time trying to make sure people understand how I feel about them," he murmured. "I am not good at explaining myself nor do I feel the need to, I guess."

"There's a certain arrogance to that. And I don't mean to be difficult all the time, though it sure seems like I am. I don't mean to," she repeated. "It's just that sometimes ... it's hard."

"I'm sure it's more than *sometimes.*" Terk smiled. "An awful lot is going on in your system that your body is dealing with. Plus, the whole emotional adjustment to the reality of becoming a parent. Not to mention hormones."

"For you as well," she admitted. "It must have been a bit of a shock to wake up and to find out that you'll be a father." He stopped in front of her room.

"I can tell you one thing for sure. I'll make a much better father than a lot of men."

"Maybe, but that's still not exactly setting the bar very high in some cases."

He tapped her on the nose. "Of all the relationships that have started among these two teams, not one of them has broken up."

"Is that even possible statistically, much less in real life?" she murmured in astonishment.

"Not only possible, it's our goal at all times."

She smiled at that. "I think I would love that."

"Come on now. Let's get you into bed."

She stumbled inside and looked up at him. "Why am I so tired?"

"I'm not sure," he admitted, "but it could be nothing more than the fact that you've had a tumultuous couple days. Now, with all that extra energy flying around in the kitchen, it could be hitting you harder than you expected."

"I didn't know what to expect, so I don't know that it could be more than I expected," she murmured, feeling a little loopy.

He chuckled. "Right. Until you've been around this kind of energy, you don't realize how much it can either drain you or charge you."

"It should charge you at all times."

"It would have, if you hadn't had your defenses up, trying to keep everybody out," he murmured softly.

She stopped and in a small voice asked, "Does everybody

know that too?"

"No. … Although my team is sharp, when it comes to love, they just shut down. They're still new at it themselves. However, don't expect them to be easy on you. And don't bother trying to keep any secrets from them."

She nodded slowly. "I wasn't so much trying to keep secrets, as I was just trying to keep some things private. I think I failed," she said, with sad smile.

"We'll get there together." And, with that, he hoped she would be satisfied. He got her to the bed and asked, "Do you want to do your teeth and stuff yet?"

"No, it's too early yet. I'll just have a quick nap."

He didn't think she had a clue how tired she really was, and, once he withdrew from this room and pulled back the energy that he'd been using to keep her upright at the table, she would crash until morning. "Maybe you should brush your teeth and get ready anyway," he suggested carefully.

She shook her head. "No, I'm fine."

When she laid down on the bed, he shrugged. "Whatever you think." She nodded, then closed her eyes. As he stepped away, he stopped at the door and frowned.

"Now what?" she whispered, without opening her eyes.

"This." And, with that, he returned to the bed and kissed her gently.

She opened her eyes and stared at him. "I feel like a two-year-old now."

"Is that so wrong?"

"No, it's just different."

"Well, different isn't always bad," he said, with a chuckle. Then he kissed her one more time, trying to clamp down the heat wanting to flare between them, and forced himself to get up and walk through the door.

"Do you think you'll find out anything tomorrow from the CIA?"

"They're notoriously difficult to communicate with in any meaningful way."

"Well, hopefully it will work out."

"That's what we're looking for, yes," he murmured. She looked over at him and frowned, but he shook his head. "Close your eyes. Get some sleep."

As he stood outside the door, he slowly withdrew his energy. When he turned around the corner, she was sound asleep. He headed back downstairs, and, as soon as he walked into the dining room, his team looked up at him.

"She really doesn't get it yet, does she?" Damon asked.

"No, but she's starting to," Terk said. "It hasn't been easy for her."

"I get that," Damon asked, "but when did this get so easy on you?"

"I don't think anybody particularly cares about what happens to me. Remember?"

"I know, and that's wrong, but hopefully she's picking up the nuances of how intertwined your futures are."

"I think she is, but our relationship is missing an awful lot of the elements that women like."

Immediately Damon nodded. "Romance. Yeah, it's a little hard under the current circumstances."

"Exactly. She's got the pregnancy, but no memories of how that happened. No memories at all, good or bad." Terk sat down. "And I think it's the unknown that is really disturbing her."

"Of course." Ice nodded sympathetically. "It would disturb anyone. We did try to convince her when she woke up that rape hadn't been involved, at least on your part, but, with no proof and you being so certain, her defenses immediately went up."

Terk looked over at Ice. "It'll be a while getting answers, but I'm hoping for some tomorrow."

At that, they set up a rough plan of what tomorrow could potentially bring and how to handle it.

If too many people were here, it would be a problem, and there was a good chance that there would be. From what Ice had been told, just two agents were coming, and they would want to go off for a walk and talk without any mic or recording devices.

Levi and Ice were notorious for recording everything, just to keep clear of trouble. But, in this case, the fact that they were meeting here meant that they would ask for that concession.

"Will you record it?" Terk asked.

"Damn right I'm recording it," she said calmly. "I'll tell them ahead of time, but, if they don't like it, I'll probably switch to a different system," she murmured.

"You really don't trust anybody, do you?"

"Do you?"

"Hell no." Terk laughed. "I'll probably still record it myself, so I can have a copy."

She chuckled. "You know I'd give you a copy,"

"Not the point. Like you, I don't trust the CIA, and I also know how machines can fail. Always good to have a backup or three."

"And what is it we're expecting tomorrow anyway?" Damon asked.

"Our old bosses are coming." Terk looked over at Damon. "And I want answers."

"What are the chances of their giving them to you?"

"We don't know yet," Terk stated calmly. "I'm pretty sure it'll be a bunch of denials."

"Of course it will," Damon murmured. "That's just what they do, isn't it?"

"It is, and it's frustrating. Hopefully we can figure out a way to get the answers we need." And, with that, Terk and his team had to be satisfied.

As he headed upstairs, he stopped at his door and frowned and walked over to her door, and he heard her inside. He knocked gently, and, when no answer came, he poked his head inside. She was thrashing on the bed, obviously disturbed about something deep in her subconscious.

He walked to her bedside and gently massaged her shoulders, until she calmed down, using energy to soothe her gently. When she took a deep sigh and settled under the covers again, he got up to head to the door.

Almost as soon as he made it to the door, she started thrashing again. Frowning, he headed back, until he sat at her bedside and waited longer before leaving. When he tried it for the third time, the same thing happened. Giving up all pretenses, he got up and went to his room, brushed his teeth, and washed up for the night. He slipped into pajama bottoms and headed to her room. When he got there, he saw the same thrashing.

He immediately climbed into bed beside her and pulled her into his arms. She calmed down instantly. While she might not know what was going on, her body sure did. So did her soul. That's the only way this connection could happen.

It was both marvelous and scary because he'd never had anybody other than his team to worry about, and now he had something even more precious. Something he'd never, ever expected to have, and that made her and these babies a gift in so many ways. And now he was desperate to keep her and their babies safe, while all the rest of his life had gone to hell and back.

CHAPTER 14

CELIA WOKE THE next morning, alone but with an indentation on the bed beside her, and she knew instinctively that Terk had been here. She could almost remember him talking to her and calming her down.

Frowning, she wondered about that. Had she'd been so neurotic in the night that he'd been forced to stay here with her?

She hoped not, but she had been pretty stressed last night. She got up, had a quick shower, and put her auburn hair into a long braid. She dressed in simple leggings and a long tunic top and headed downstairs.

Today was the meeting with the CIA, but she didn't know when it was. As she looked down at the time on the cell phone that Ice had given her, once she'd regained consciousness, it was already nine.

She walked into the dining room via the door closest to the coffeepot, then noted an odd tension in the room behind her. She slowly looked over her shoulder to see the two new arrivals, amid Terk's team and Levi and Ice. The meeting had effectively started. She looked to Terk for reassurance, but his gaze was on the CIA men. "Oops," she said lightly, "looks like I interrupted something."

"You did," one of the men said, his tone brisk. "You can leave anytime."

But his tone reminded her of too many who she had worked with at her labs, not to mention those involved in grants and other such donations. She shook her head. "No, I don't think so." Then she walked over and pulled out the empty chair beside Terk and sat down. She slipped one hand under the table and grabbed his. He immediately held on to hers but didn't say a word.

The rude man looked at her in surprise.

She added, "I'm another person badly affected by this whole scenario. I want answers too, so I won't be going anywhere."

"How are you affected?"

She stood up, showing him her baby bump. When he frowned in confusion, she clarified, "I was kidnapped off the street, drugged, and held captive, God-only-knows where, and inseminated with Terk's sperm," she stated boldly. "Then I was wired up with C-4, and I was dumped outside this compound. So, any answers you have for them, also are due to me."

He stared at her, and his jaw dropped. "Jesus, seriously?" He looked around at Ice.

Ice nodded. "Seriously, and we have her arrival on tape."

"Good God," he murmured. "Nothing like that was ever supposed to happen." He said it in such a low whisper, yet it was audible to Celia. She leaned forward. "If it wasn't *supposed* to happen, maybe you'd explain just how it *was* supposed to happen."

He looked at her. "I didn't say anything."

"Yes, you did," she snapped. "You just stated, *It wasn't supposed to happen like that.*"

At that, Terk stiffened beside her, but he didn't look at her. And she was grateful because she believed—at least at this point in time—that he trusted her that much.

The man glared at her. "I don't know what you're talking about," he snarled. "Don't go putting words in my mouth."

"*I* don't have to. *You* said it," she snapped. "And don't call me a liar because that won't go over well. Now, the truth, please." She glared at him. When he didn't answer, she added, "It's really in your best interests to talk because no way in hell you want to be bucking up against a pregnant woman who's very unstable and quite pissed off." Her voice was hard, as she glared at him. "Right now, you're looking like my best bet for getting answers."

He just stared at her, and his jaw worked.

She risked a glance over at Terk, but his lips twitched, and she relaxed ever-so-slightly. She returned her hard gaze to the man sitting in front of her. Then slipped a glance to the second CIA guy, who was sitting back, a sneer on his face, and she caught something coming from his energy too.

She frowned. "What the hell?" She stared at the second man, then back at the first. "This guy is laughing at you for being on the spot, thinking he'd never be such an idiot to get himself in that position. You do know that, right?"

He glared at her, then turned to look at his cohort, who was now looking at her, stunned.

Celia had made it sound like it was just a guess, but she knew exactly what he was thinking. And what a surprise that was. "Yeah, I'm really good at reading facial expressions."

"You run a shady business, dealing in testing psychics," the second man bit off. "So don't try any of that bullshit with me."

"Oh, right, because you're so much better than everybody else here. I got it," she said, with a sneer right back at him. "What are you even doing here, considering you didn't want to come?"

"How do you know I didn't want to come?"

"The look on your face says you don't want to be here. That you don't want anything to do with this."

"Of course I don't want anything to do with it. Everything should have had been terminated by now."

"And I wonder what you mean by that," she murmured, as she studied him. She caught an ever-so-slight whisper of something in his features.

She squeezed Terk's hand, and he squeezed back in support, but he still remained silent. She wasn't sure what was happening with her today, but, maybe because she was connected to Terk, she was now getting thoughts from other people.

Regardless she was reading this second guy loud and clear, and she realized that he didn't like her one bit. "Yeah, it's too damn bad that you don't like me. I won't lose any sleep over it."

He stiffened and glared at her. "What the hell? Are you just a mouthpiece? What are you even doing here?"

"You'd be surprised," Celia said calmly, as she studied him. "Man, you're such a loser."

He stared at her in shock.

"Oops." She smiled. "That's what you're thinking about your buddy here."

His buddy turned and looked at him. "Seriously? Is that what you're doing? How about a little support here?"

"It's been a fuckup since the beginning," he snapped, staring at Celia. "We're just trying to salvage our way out of this."

"No salvaging to be had," she said cheerfully to Terk and

the others. "I mean, this guy's been behind it since the beginning."

"Like hell I was," the second guy roared.

"You were," she murmured. "You and Leopold."

"Leopold? What about him?" asked the first man in confusion.

She looked at the two CIA agents and asked, "Which one of you is Grady?" Then she looked at the sneering man and nodded. "You're Grady."

At that, Terk nodded too. "That's the connection. You're the one who was behind it all. You're the one who thinks this should have been done *properly*."

"It *should* have been done properly," he sneered. "The whole division should have been terminated properly. I've been saying that since the beginning. That's nothing new."

"Except your idea of *properly terminated* is to *permanently terminate*," Terk said.

His team started to mumble, but Celia kept her gaze on Grady. And something else was there that she didn't like one bit—a confidence on his face that he had no right to have. He was not fazed by this. "And you didn't come alone, did you, Grady?" She took a stab in the dark.

"Of course I didn't." He gave her a negligent shrug. "I came with him obviously."

"And you're hoping to use him as a patsy to get yourself out of this."

"I don't need to use him for anything. He's my boss."

"But you were not allowed a say in how this division needed to be taken down, were you?"

"No, of course not," Grady said, disinterested. "Yet the higher-ups all knew better. You can't just eliminate their jobs like a traditional layoff and expect them to really go away."

Just enough of his condescending tone filled his voice to make her realize he didn't think much of the CIA's methodology at all.

"And, as far as you're concerned, your bosses failed and don't deserve a second chance, especially since they wouldn't listen to you from the beginning," Celia stated.

He stared at her. "Who the hell are you?"

"Nobody. Remember that. I'm just some nobody who was testing psychics before all this," she said, with an eye roll.

"Well then, shut the fuck up," he growled, his voice hard.

She stiffened. "Don't you dare talk to me like that."

"Or what?"

She got up, walked over to him. "Did you just say that?" She wasn't sure what she was even doing, but she was so pissed at him right now.

Terk immediately stood and joined her, reaching out to grab her gently. "Calm down. He's just being a fool. He probably can't help himself."

"No, he's creating a diversion," she snapped. "His energy keeps going off in a million directions, as he tries to pull things together. He's waiting for something, and he doesn't know how long it'll take."

At that, Ice looked at her in surprise and walked out of the dining room.

Celia sat back down again. "Don't even talk to me. There is nothing I want to hear from you."

"Good," he said, with an eye roll, "the psych ward is waiting."

"Yeah, I'm sure you'd have fun with that," she murmured. "Just remember this. If I wanted to send you to a psych ward, it would take me only a few moments. A little tweak here, a little tweak there, and *boom*. The mind is a fragile thing, Grady. Too bad it won't be necessary."

"Hey, by the time we're done with you, you'll be locked up in a padded room, and your baby opted out," he snapped, his voice hard.

"Ah." She gave him a headshake. "I wouldn't be so confident, if I were you."

The first man looked at her and then faced his partner. "Grady, what the hell?"

"Come on. They're just playing you, Alan," Grady said. "You know perfectly well that Terk has outlived his usefulness. Levi too, as far as I'm concerned. How many times have these people been in the middle of shitstorms all over the world, then expect us to just clean it up for them, while they ride off into the sunset? Too many times. It's a pain in the ass. They cause nothing but trouble, and we need to shut them down."

"Yeah? You and how many others?" Stone asked, walking into the room, his arms crossed over his chest. "Are you talking about the militia group trying to get onto the property?"

At that, Levi looked over at Grady. "Grady, is that true?"

"We're calling in our markers." Grady nodded. He looked over at Alan, who stared at him in shock. "You're such a loser, Alan. By the way, you've been fired by the CIA. You don't run this department anymore. I do." Then he stood. "When the men get in here, they'll take you back to town, Alan. You will go through a debriefing, then either be reassigned within the agency or formally let go."

"Jesus, Grady," Alan cried out. "What the hell have you done?"

"What you should have done in the first place," he

snapped. "These assholes should never have been allowed to run free like this. The whole department was a bad deal right from the beginning, and the minute we started to talk about shutting them down, we should have done it permanently."

"Is that what you did?" Terk asked, looking over at Grady. "Are you the one who decided to take matters into your own hands?"

"Doesn't matter if I am," Grady replied. "I had a perfect weapon to use."

"The Iranians."

He shrugged. "The same team that you supposedly took out. But, in typical fuck-up fashion, you left one alive."

"We know," Terk agreed. "That one's now dead too. His brother is gone as well. There really isn't anybody left anymore. Did you sanction all these deaths too?" Terk looked over at Alan, before he continued. "In which case you've got no business being upset at us over bodies."

Alan still stared at his cohort. "What the hell have you done, Grady?" he cried out, standing up and facing him.

"Only what you should have done. I just told you that," Grady snarled. "We hired the Iranians to close out a contract on these guys and used their newly designed weapon that we've been working on for a long time. This gave us a chance to try it out. It was supposed to beat these guys, and we wouldn't need anything else."

"Yes, but the prototype didn't work." Alan stared at him. "You know that."

"Well, it seems they had a duplicate that they kept to themselves," Grady noted calmly. "And we decided that it could work just fine, with a little modification."

"*We?*" Terk pounced. "Who's the *we* in this?"

"Doesn't matter. Nobody in this room will survive past

today anyway."

"Says you." Levi stared him down. "Do you really think we're such idiots that we would let you in here without first ensuring we were safe?"

"Doesn't matter if you're safe or not." Grady laughed. "You morons still don't understand."

"Oh, I think I understand plenty." Levi stood. He looked over at Alan. "What about you, Alan? You got enough?"

"Oh, I've got enough all right." Alan shook his head. "Jesus Christ, Grady. How many people did you kill in this process?"

"*I* didn't kill anybody." Grady shrugged. "And the rest was just collateral damage. You should have known it would be a problem leaving these guys alive, and look at them. Look at the bodies they have left strewn everywhere. It didn't have to be that way, if you would have just listened to me in the first place."

"What will you do about it now?" Levi asked, with a smile. "You didn't bring a weapon into the building, and none of your cohorts outside have access to us, unless we allow them inside."

"They've got all your *accesses* controlled." Grady gave Levi an ugly smile. "They're coming in the way you least expect them to."

"No, they aren't," Ice said, returning to the room. "They've all been taken captive and are safely secured in our jail. You may want to come and have a look."

Grady shrugged. "Good idea. I intend to take a prisoner from you anyway." Then as a group, with Grady in tow, they walked down to the compound's jail. It was full. At that, Grady swore. "What the hell?" he roared. "What the hell did you do?"

"We took them all prisoner, just like I told you," Ice said, her voice cold as her name.

"They were trespassing," Levi stated calmly, "and of course they were heavily armed."

Outside, they heard helicopters arriving. "What the hell is that?" Grady spun around. "Release these men," he ordered, "and I mean now."

"Hell no." Levi crossed his arms over his chest. "I don't do anything just because you tell me to."

"I said, release them."

At the same time that Grady stepped forward, one of the team looked at him and shook his head. "I don't think that'll work."

"It won't," Terk confirmed, as he walked up to Grady, and, with his right fist, clocked him in the face, hard. Grady dropped to the floor, unconscious. Terk turned and looked at Alan. "You've got one chance."

"This had nothing to do with me," he said, holding up his hands. "Honest. I didn't know anything about this."

"Well, it sounds to me as if it's time for you to find out every last detail. And one chance—one chance only—to set this right."

CHAPTER 15

C ELIA CHEERED TERK on, as he dropped Grady to the floor.

Everybody stared at her in surprise.

"What? I wouldn't miss this." She snorted. "That asshole needed to be taken down a notch or two." She glared at the rest of them in the jail. "If you're with him, I'm totally okay letting Terk pop every one of you."

At that, Alan laughed. "Not necessary. I'll be taking all these men back with me," he stated in a crisp voice. He looked down at the man on the ground. "Really disappointed in you, Grady."

"Maybe so"—he slowly opened his eyes—"but, if you think you'll survive the inquiry into this, you're wrong."

"Says you," Alan replied. "You did all this without being sanctioned."

"We are sanctioned," called out a voice from inside the cells. "We all are."

Alan frowned at him. "Because this guy says so?"

"No," another voice interrupted, "because I said so."

As Alan turned, he came face-to-face with his boss.

Terk stepped back ever-so-slightly. "Leopold, I presume?"

Behind him was Stone, and, as Levi looked over at the rest of them, he saw his team positioned throughout the room.

"So, you wanted us all dead, is that it?" Terk asked.

"It did seem to be the best idea. Look at you." He made an exaggerated wave of his hand. "You obviously won't be a team that we can kill easily, so we might as well reopen the damn department again."

"Oh, I don't think so," Terk stated calmly, as he studied him. "You know, for us, that requires trust, something that we obviously don't have with you guys, since you're the ones who tried to kill us."

"Yeah, we sure did." Leopold shook his head. "We ordered a hit on you to test this new weapon that was supposed to be the new greatest thing to use against our enemies. See how well that worked."

Terk snorted. "More bullshit."

"Well, everybody is full of bullshit at some point."

"We weren't." Terk studied the room, looking as though he was wondering what he was supposed to do with this scenario.

"No," Leopold agreed, "you weren't, and that's why I want to reopen the department."

"No. That's not the plan," Grady shouted.

"Shut up, Grady. This is your mess that I'm trying to clean up here. So, Terk, what'll it be?"

"The answer is no." Terk shook his head.

"Well, in that case, I'll ask the rest of your team," he murmured. "I'm sure some of them would be happy to come back and set this to rights."

"And why would they do that?" Terk asked, clearly not buying it.

And, at that, Leopold laughed. "Well, if you really think you're getting out of this whole and healthy," he said, "you might want to take a look at this." And, with that, he held up a tablet, showing the rest of his team in England, standing under armed guard, with all the women prominently in the photo, even Little Calum. Leopold held it out for the rest of the team to see.

"You son of a bitch," Calum cried out, stepping forward.

"We've got the rest of your team," Leopold stated. "So, either come back into the fold or we'll take you all out."

"Well, that would be one way to go," Terk replied, "but you're here in Levi's compound. Do you really think taking out my team is the right move? Of course, if you want to get out alive yourself, you *will* have to take the rest of us down."

"No, you see? Levi and Ice have been causing us headaches for a long time. Either this happens, and he keeps his mouth shut, or his team will go down too," Leopold said calmly.

At that, Terk looked over at Levi, who was burning with fury. "Wow, Leopold," Terk noted, "you've bitten off more than I think you can chew."

"I am the damn boss," he yelled. "I shouldn't even have to be here. That's my helicopter outside."

"Really?" Terk murmured. "We've never dealt with you before."

"That's because I'm above all you assholes," he explained, with a wave of his hand. "Normally I wouldn't even be involved, but, due to the sensitive nature of this mess, here I am. We've got to clean this up, once and for all."

"So, who's above you?" Terk asked.

"What difference does that make? I run everything, and what I say goes."

At that, Ice held up her phone, recording the interchange. She was also live streaming to the defense department. "Wouldn't that be Brigadier General Smithson?"

He looked over at her cell phone screen, and his face twisted in rage. "Listen, girlie. Do you really think videotaping this will make a fucking bit of difference? That's why I'm here. I came to make sure we clean this mess up, once and for all."

Immediately the brigadier general's voice came through Ice's phone, loud and clear. "Leopold, you miserable asshole, this is your boss, Smithson. I am so damn tired of you going behind my back, meddling in things that are none of your fucking business. This was not a sanctioned mission, nor was the ill-fated attempt to take out Terk's team."

"Well, if he wasn't your bloody pet," Leopold roared, "I wouldn't have had to fix their screwups."

"They didn't screw up, you moron. In fact, they were doing a hell of a job. You took it upon yourself to close down the organization without approval, and, if that weren't enough, you committed countless crimes in the process. You had no business doing any of that. I can't even begin to fathom the body count you've got in this mess, but I damn well will find out, and I'll hold your ass accountable."

"No way we'll let a weapon like this team live," Leopold sneered, "and the same goes for your pets, Levi and Ice. No way I'm letting them go." He raised his hand. "And by the way, General, if you didn't see the hidden signals before now, see this one, and let the bloodshed begin." And, with that, he dropped his arm.

There was, indeed, a signal, followed by a single gunshot—but it was Grady who took the bullet between his eyes. At that, Alan stepped forward, faced Ice's phone. "Brigadier General, sir, Grady has been taken out," Alan said, fatigue in his voice. "You'll need a team to come in here."

"Yeah, well, Leopold's team is outside, standing by. They are not privy to this madness and are the team you'll need," he snapped. "I've vetted every one of those men. Get that cleaned up and bring everybody home, and I want that fucker Leopold in chains. I need to find out what else he's had his fingers in. Grady was just a bad seed, Alan. He had to go. Don't lose any sleep over that. Levi and Ice, I'll talk to you soon. And Terk, damn, son, I'm sorry."

"Yeah, me too. We'll talk later."

"You bet." He hesitated and added, "I guess you're serious about not wanting to reopen the team, huh?"

"We're going private, sir," Terk said adamantly.

"That's not a bad idea. A lot of money in contracts these days."

"There is," Terk agreed, "but that's not what I'm after. It'll be on our terms, with our own systems and defenses."

"Will you stay there with Levi and Ice?"

"No, sir, we'll set up in England," he said, hearing the mood behind him lift. "And the team has doubled in size in recent weeks."

"Shit, man, you got that many psychics now?"

"We're growing all the time, sir," Terk replied. "We're stronger than ever, so we'll talk down the road. Make sure your pockets are deep."

"Yeah, about that. You want to talk about the money that was in your budget and now isn't?"

"We needed that money to save our asses from Leopold and his goons. Not to mention Grady."

At that, the brigadier general chuckled. "You know what? That is fair. We'll let that one bury itself in paperwork."

"Good enough." Terk smiled. "I'm heading back to England in a few days. We'll talk then." And, as Ice shut down that call, Terk picked up Leopold's phone. "Clary? How are you doing over there? We're fine here."

She said, "We just had to wait until it was over."

"The guards?"

"Dead." She shrugged. "No one who is willing to hurt women and children gets a second chance."

"Yeah," Wade said. "Besides, anything that pisses off MI6 will make us happy."

Raising an eyebrow, Terk snorted at that. "We need to get them on our side somehow. To have one government on our side is gold, but two? ... Well, that's a hell of a lot better." He addressed his team. "Well?"

"Oh, we're good." Damon grinned at him. "We're totally good with going independent."

"You okay with England?" Terk's gaze swept his four men who had come over and received nods all around. Then he turned to Ice and Levi. "You guys will be okay?"

"Always," Levi said calmly. "Don't you worry about us."

"It just took forever to get these guys to show us their hand," Ice added.

And, with that, Terk nodded. He looked over at Celia. "Is England okay?"

She raised her eyebrows. "Thanks for *asking*," she quipped, with an emphasis on the *asking* part. "But, as long as I have a place to raise my twins, that's fine with me."

"Good, and I wasn't asking. It was out of politeness that I was doing that much."

She glared at him. "We need to work on your manners."

"No. However, you can if you feel like it, but I'd give up

on lost causes."

She groaned. "You don't have to be difficult about everything."

"Not everything." He grinned at her. "Just some things."

And when he laughed at her, she realized she was being teased.

At that, he noted the question in her gaze. "And?"

"Are you serious about setting up your own team again?" Celia asked.

"The team never disbanded," Terk said. "Not really. We had plans to briefly go our separate ways, then found each other in the face of a crisis, so we're all trying to figure out what to do next. It will take some time to get ourselves set up. We haven't even had time to plan, but we can all do it, together."

"Well, maybe good things can come out of this after all," Celia murmured.

He nodded, looked over to his team members, and they were all smiles. "In a couple days we're heading back."

"Right," Damon agreed. They all were looking hopeful. "We need to get back home, then do some real planning."

"We do, indeed," Terk murmured. "At least now we officially have the budget to do so."

"So," Ice interrupted, "do I get to ask how much budget money was in that account that you're now keeping with their permission?" Ice was curious and just a little bit envious.

"Nope." He walked over and enveloped her in a big hug. "But, if you ever need anything, you know you can always call on us."

"Absolutely," Levi agreed, rubbing his hands together. "Man, now we'll have a sister company in England too.

That's just about perfect."

"That's what I said. And Terk and his team can help smooth things over with MI6," Ice reminded Levi.

Levi almost chortled with joy when he heard that. "This is just about perfect." Levi looked over at the rest of them. "I don't know about you guys, but, once this criminal lot has been cleared out of here, I think it should be pool time."

"Absolutely," Ice agreed. "And drinks," she added, with feeling.

"And maybe more food," Celia said suddenly.

They all looked at her, and she shrugged. "Hey, I'm pregnant. With twins no less. What can I say?"

The laughter was loud and universal. As Terk tucked her up into his arms, he said, "Come on. ... Maybe you should have a nap first."

"I don't need a nap." She frowned, but he shook his head.

"You absolutely do. Your energy is just about to plummet."

"You must be draining it then."

"If I'm draining your energy, it's only because I've been supporting you, and now I need to recharge myself." She turned and looked at him, and he nodded. She sighed. "Damn, I thought I was doing much better."

"You were. However, if you're planning on heading to the pool and joining the rest of us for the evening," he said, "you need to get some rest first."

CELIA GROANED AND followed him obediently into her room. Instead he took her into his room, and she glared at him suspiciously. "What are we—"

Immediately he covered her mouth with his lips.

And once again that same firestorm overtook her, causing all her senses to vibrate. When she pulled her mouth free, she stated, "You won't be able to overwhelm me with your kisses all the time, you know?"

"Not all the time." He pulled her back into his arms, lowering his lips. "Just whenever the need arises."

She snorted at that. "As long as it's concerning *both* of our needs."

He kissed her deep and long, and, when he lifted his head, he asked, "What do you think? Does it meet both of our needs?"

"God, yes." She grabbed his ears and pulled him down to her.

He burst out laughing, until their lips touched, and, as the laughter subsided, the passion rose.

By the time she stepped back and got her shirt over her head, he'd already chucked his jeans and stood in front of her, completely nude.

She stared at him in awe. "Good God," she whispered. "You're not only a bloody escape artist but you got out of those clothes faster than anybody I've ever seen before. ... And you're absolutely gorgeous."

He stared at her and shook his head. "Hell no. I'm a broken, aging, and outdated warrior."

She placed a finger against his lips. "No, you're an incredibly good man, who has lived through endless wars and come out on the other side, stronger than before. And, for that, I am absolutely delighted."

He helped her take off the rest of her clothes at a much gentler pace. A little slower but not too much, as she could feel the tension coiling deep within her. "Jesus," she murmured, as he carried her to the bed. "It's never been anything like this."

"I think that's what happens when you find the other half of your soul," he murmured. "I might not be any good at showing my feelings or using flowery phrases, but what I say comes from my heart. And you are the other half of mine. You just need to give yourself time to feel it too."

She stopped, struck by the simple poetry and the absolute sincerity in his voice. In that moment, she realized there would never be romance from somebody like Terk, but there would be sincerity that came from the heart, with words that came out of the blue, like those just spoken. And they were worth everything to her.

"I don't need time," she whispered. "I felt it but was too scared to acknowledge it." With tears in her eyes, she wrapped him up in a warm hug and whispered, "I hope it's always like this."

"It will be if we make it that way," he murmured, "with communication, love, and us—all the tools in the toolbox of making a great relationship. Effort is the other part that goes into it, and I think we've got that sewn up tight." He wrapped her up close and proceeded to demonstrate just how well they had that wrapped up.

Soon she was gasping and trembling on the bed, her thighs wide, begging him to come to her. He slowly slid up, until he was right in position.

"I don't want to hurt you," he said, his fingers still teasing her, until she was writhing.

"You won't hurt me."

"What about the babies?"

"You won't hurt them either," she said. "I was made for

this." Her voice was dark, thick, and deep with passion, and, when he still hesitated, she wrapped her legs around his thighs and tugged him over her, then plunged herself upward, so he went in deep and hard.

He sank even lower and dropped his forehead gently against hers and whispered, "God, that's incredible."

"It's amazing."

And then he started to move, and everything that she thought she knew about making love went out the window.

It was incredible.

It was tumultuous.

It was almost painful because she was on a knife's edge of something momentous, but, at the same time, she knew something else was missing.

He whispered, "Open up your mind." She frowned at him. "Do it," he said.

Immediately she opened the door that he had shown her, and he stepped through.

She could really see him now, with *all* her senses involved, the same as he could see her. Souls, not bodies. Energy, minds, hearts—as one. "Oh my God," she whispered. They were joined on a level that she had never dreamed possible. By the time she exploded in his arms, she already knew he was there, holding her energy, her heart, her soul, and carrying her with him.

He carried her over the edge, the two of them, forever bonded together.

EPILOGUE

ALMOST ONE MONTH later, as they landed in London, Celia winced because her lower back and the long flight had not been a good combination.

"You and the babies okay?" Terk murmured, as he ushered her toward the big SUV waiting for them.

"Yep." She yawned heavily. "They're both more than ready to rest though, and so am I."

"Lots of rest coming up," he murmured.

"We still don't have a home yet," she said, looking at him.

"Depends on how you feel about being part of a big compound."

"Like Ice and Levi's?"

He chuckled. "Yeah. Something like that."

As they drove out of town, she thought about a compound and what that would be like as a home, a working home. But when the drive went a little longer than expected, she turned and asked, "Where are we going?"

"Charles suggested a new place as a base. I've been there before, but I didn't realize it was up for sale."

"What kind of a place is it?"

He looked over at her, as they started to climb a mountain. "How do you feel about something fairly old-fashioned?"

She frowned. "As long as it's got all the modern ameni-
ties—you know, inside plumbing, hot water, electricity, and
communications—I don't hate the idea, especially if it's got
some history and charm."

He laughed, as they entered through a huge stone wall
and a double gate.

She looked at him in shock. "Oh my God. Is this a castle?"

"Kind of." Terk chuckled. "It looks like it might be big
enough for the expanding family."

"What is there, like twenty of us or something?" she
asked.

"So far, nineteen, counting the twins. Plus, we'll need
people to help run the place, like weapons specialists,
builders, tech support, culinary staff, housekeeping, garden-
ers, and whatever else. We'll need a bunch of staff, unless
you've got a problem with that."

She stared at the unfolding landscape, as they drove
around and came into full view of the castle, and she was just
stunned. "Is that a moat?" she cried out in delight, as the
grassy grounds went straight to the water's edge. She
bounced out of the SUV and raced over to the water in an
awkwardly pregnant hop.

"I see you approve of it, but I don't think the twins appreciate the bouncing."

She laughed, holding her belly. "Is there a pool too?"

"There is a pool. Now, we haven't finalized any of the
legal arrangements yet, but the plan is to spend a few days
here, while we think about it."

"What's to think about?" she cried out, turning to look
at him in shock. "Sign on the dotted line. I think it's
perfect."

He had to admit that he thought so too. As he looked around at the grounds, he could envision them all here.

She whispered, "Can we really afford this?"

"We can afford it, especially since the US government has paid for it," he said, chuckling.

"Well, considering that they tried to kill us all, and we could have had them caught up in litigation for decades and would have gotten the money anyway," she murmured, "it's pretty much all good."

"Exactly, so, in theory, we've just saved them money." He reached out for her hand. "Come on. Let's go take a look at our new home."

Just then the front door opened, and an older man leaned against the door, a gentle smile on his face.

"Charles?" Terk said in delight. "I wasn't expecting to see you here."

He nodded, beaming at Terk and Celia. "Not sure how you feel about it, but I thought I'd meet you here and make sure everything was in order."

The men shook hands, and Terk introduced Celia to Charles. She was immediately drawn to the charming older man. "It's very nice to meet you, and I hope you'll stay." She was filled with joy, as she reached out and hugged him, already enjoying the kind energy of this man.

Charles flushed with pleasure. "How sweet of you. I do have a friend here with me." Celia watched as an older woman walked—with an obvious limp—toward them along the long central hallway.

As the men stepped away to look at something on the property, the woman approached Celia and smiled, holding out her hand. "Hello, I am Emmeline. Charles and I are old school friends."

"So nice to meet you. I'm Celia." She couldn't take her eyes off the woman, immediately noting that Emmeline was the type who only grew more beautiful with age.

"This is such a beautiful and peaceful place. I already want to visit again," Emmeline replied.

"Absolutely." Celia hugged the woman. She looked over at Terk, as he and Charles returned. "I don't think anybody here will mind, and the place looks to be huge. I hope we can get it."

"Oh, wait until you see inside it," Emmaline said. "It's amazing."

"Perfect." Celia beamed. "All I want to do now is explore, and then I want to hit that pool, wherever it is."

Charles laughed. "It's being uncovered right now. It should be ready within the hour, so probably about the time the tour is complete," he said affectionately. "I also took the liberty of having a meal prepared."

Celia grinned at him. "I knew I liked you already." She reached out to grab Terk's hand. "Come on, Terk. Our future is waiting." *The pool is also waiting for us*, she whispered in his mind.

What about the twins?

They can handle it. So can we.

This concludes Book 8 of Terkel's Team: Terkel's Twist.

Read about Terkel's Triumph: Terkel's Team, Book 9

Terkel's Team: Terkel's Triumph (Book #9)

Welcome to a brand-new series from *USA Today* best-selling author Dale Mayer, where dark-ops SEALs have special senses and skills, needed to solve intrigue, betrayal, and … murder. A series with all the elements you've come to love, plus so much more, … including psychics!

The move to a castle is both daunting and exhilarating. Damn sure he has bitten of more than he can handle, Terk asks Charles for help. In turn, Charles brings in an old friend to get the team installed and to get the castle renovated and organized. Going into private business never looked so good or so hard. But, with Levi and Ice joining in the fun, even Bullard helping out, the renovations are in Emmaline's capable hands, and all is well.

Or is it? When Jonas calls to say there's a problem, and it's heading their way, Terk knows the priority is safety and security. But what does that look like with a large group of energy workers? There's also another side effect of so much energy all in one place—something no one thought about—

and something that's way too late to stop …

Find Book 9 here!

To find out more visit Dale Mayer's website.

https://geni.us/DMTTTriumphUniversal

Magnus: Shadow Recon (Book #1)

Deep in the permafrost of the Arctic, a joint task force, comprised of over one dozen countries, comes together to level up their winter skills. A mix of personalities, nationalities, and egos bring out the best—and the worst—as these globally elite men and women work and play together. They rub elbows with hardy locals and a group of scientists gathered close by …

One fatality is almost expected with this training. A second is tough but not a surprise. However, when a third goes missing? It's hard to not be suspicious. When the missing man is connected to one of the elite Maverick team members and is a special friend of Lieutenant Commander Mason Callister? All hell breaks loose …

LIEUTENANT COMMANDER MASON Callister walked into the private office and stood in front of retired Navy Commander Doran Magellan.

"Mason, good to see you."

Yet the dry tone of voice, and the scowl pinching the silver-haired man, all belied his words. Mason had known Doran for over a decade, and their friendship had only grown over time.

Mason waited, as he watched the other man try to work the new tech phone system on his desk. With his hand circling the air above the black box, he appeared to hit buttons randomly.

Mason held back his amusement but to no avail.

"Why can't a phone be a phone anymore?" the commander snapped, as his glare shifted from Mason to the box and back.

Asking the commander if he needed help wouldn't make the older man feel any better, but sitting here and watching as he indiscriminately punched buttons was a struggle. "Is Helen away?" Mason asked.

"Yes, damn it. She's at lunch, and I need her to be at lunch." The commander's piercing gaze pinned Mason in place. "No one is to know you're here."

Solemn, Mason nodded. "Understood."

"Doran? Is that you?" A crotchety voice slammed into the room through the phone's speakers. "Get away from that damn phone. You keep clicking buttons in my ear. Get

Helen in there to do this."

"No, she can't be here for this."

Silence came first, then a huge groan. "Damn it. Then you should have connected me last, so I don't have to sit here and listen to you fumbling around."

"Go pour yourself a damn drink then," Doran barked. "I'm working on the others."

A snort was his only response.

Mason bit the inside of his lip, as he really tried to hold back his grin. The retired commander had been hell on wheels while on active duty, and, even now, the retired part of his life seemed to be more of a euphemism than anything.

"Damn things …"

Mason looked around the dark mahogany office and the walls filled with photos, awards, medals. A life of purpose, accomplishment. And all of that had only piqued his interest during the initial call he'd received, telling him to be here at this time.

"Ah, got it."

Mason's eyebrows barely twitched, as the commander gave him a feral grin. "I'd rather lead a warship into battle than deal with some of today's technology."

As he was one of only a few commanders who'd been in a position to do such a thing, it said much about his capabilities.

And much about current technology.

The commander leaned back in his massive chair and motioned to the cart beside Mason. "Pour three cups."

Interesting. Mason walked a couple steps across the rich tapestry-style carpet and lifted the silver service to pour coffee into three very down-to-earth-looking mugs.

"Black for me."

Mason picked up two cups and walked one over to Doran.

"Thanks." He leaned forward and snapped into the phone, "Everyone here?"

Multiple voices responded.

Curiouser and curiouser. Mason recognized several of the voices. Other relics of an era gone by. Although not a one would like to hear that, and, in good faith, it wasn't fair. Mason had thought each of these men were retired, had relinquished power. Yet, as he studied Doran in front of him, Mason had to wonder if any of them actually had passed the baton or if they'd only slid into the shadows. Was this planned with the government's authority? Or were these retirees a shadow group to the government?

The tangible sense of power and control oozed from Doran's words, tone, stature—his very pores. This man might be heading into his sunset years—based on a simple calculation of chronological years spent on the planet—but he was a long way from being out of the action.

"Mason ..." Doran began.

"Sir?"

"We've got a problem."

Mason narrowed his gaze and waited.

Doran's glare was hard, steely hard, with an icy glint. "Do you know the Mavericks?"

Mason's eyebrows shot up. The black ops division was one of those well-kept secrets, so, therefore, everyone knew about it. He gave a decisive nod. "I do."

"And you're involved in the logistics behind the ICE training program in the Arctic, are you not?"

"I am." Now where was the commander going with this?

"Do you know another SEAL by the name of Mountain

Rode? He's been working for the black ops Mavericks." At his own words, the commander shook his head. "What the hell was his mother thinking when she gave him that moniker?"

"She wasn't thinking anything," said the man with a hard voice from behind Mason.

He stiffened slightly, then relaxed as he recognized that voice too.

"She died giving birth to me. And my full legal name is Mountain Bear Rode. It was my father's doing."

The commander glared at the new arrival. "Did I say you could come in?"

"Yes." Mountain's voice was firm, yet a definitive note of affection filled his tone.

That emotion told Mason so much.

The commander harrumphed, then cleared his throat. "Mason, we're picking up a significant amount of chatter over that ICE training. Most of it good. Some of it the usual caterwauling we've come to expect every time we participate in a joint training mission. This one is set to run for six months, then to reassess."

Mason already knew this. But he waited for the commander to get around to why Mason was here, and, more important, what any of this had to do with the mountain of a man who now towered beside him.

The commander shifted his gaze to Mountain, but he remained silent.

Mason noted Mountain was not only physically big but damn imposing and severely pissed, seemingly barely holding back the forces within. His body language seemed to yell, *And the world will fix this, or I'll find the reason why.*

For a moment Mason felt sorry for the world.

Finally a voice spoke through the phone. "Mason, this is Alpha here. I run the Mavericks. We've got a problem with that ICE training center. Mountain, tell him."

Mason shifted to include Mountain in his field of vision. Mason wished the other men on the conference call were in the room too. It was one thing to deal with men you knew and could take the measure of; it was another when they were silent shadows in the background.

"My brother is one of the men who reported for the Artic training three weeks ago."

"Tergan Rode?" Mason confirmed. "I'm the one who arranged for him to go up there. He's a great kid."

A glimmer of a smile cracked Mountain's stony features. He nodded. "Indeed. A bright light in my often dark world. He's a dozen years younger than me, just passed his BUD/s training this spring, and raring to go. Until his raring to go then got up and went."

Oh, shit. Mason's gaze zinged to the commander, who had kicked up his feet to rest atop the big desk. Stocking feet. With Mickey Mouse images dancing on them. Sidetracked, Mason struggled to pull his attention back to Mountain. "Meaning?"

"He's disappeared." Mountain let out a harsh breath, as if just saying that out loud, and maybe to the right people, could allow him to relax—at least a little.

The commander spoke up. "We need your help, Mason. You're uniquely qualified for this problem."

It didn't sound like he was qualified in any way for anything he'd heard so far. "Clarify." His spoken word was simplicity itself, but the tone behind it said he wanted the cards on the table ... now.

Mountain spoke up. "He's the third incident."

Mason's gaze narrowed, as the reports from the training

camp rolled through his mind. "One was Russian. One was from the German SEAL team. Both were deemed accidental deaths."

"No, they weren't."

There it was. The root of the problem in black-and-white. He studied Mountain, aiming for neutrality. "Do you have evidence?"

"My brother did."

"Ah, hell."

Mountain gave a clipped nod. "I'm going to find him."

"Of that I have no doubt," Mason said quietly. "Do you have a copy of the evidence he collected?"

"I have some of it." Mountain held out a USB key. "This is your copy. Top secret."

"We don't have to remind you, Mason, that lives are at stake," Doran added. "Nor do we need another international incident. Consider also that a group of scientists, studying global warming, is close by, and not too far away is a village home to a few hardy locals."

Mason accepted the key, turned to the commander, and asked, "Do we know if this is internal or enemy warfare?"

"We don't know at this point," Alpha replied through the phone. "Mountain will lead Shadow Recon. His mission is twofold. One, find out what's behind these so-called accidents and put a stop to it by any means necessary. Two, locate his brother, hopefully alive."

"And where do I come in?" Mason asked.

"We want you to pull together a special team. The members of Shadow Recon will report to both you and Mountain, just in case."

That was clear enough.

"You'll stay stateside but in constant communication with Mountain—with the caveat that, if necessary, you're on the next flight out."

"What about bringing in other members from the Mavericks?" Mason suggested.

Alpha took this question too, his response coming through via Speakerphone. "We don't have the numbers. The budget for our division has been cut. So we called the commander to pull some strings."

That was Doran's cue to explain further. "Mountain has fought hard to get me on board with this plan, and I'm here now. The navy has a special budget for Shadow Recon and will take care of Mountain and you, Mason, and the team you provide."

"Skills needed?"

"Everything," Mountain said, his voice harsh. "But the biggest is these men need to operate in the shadows, mostly alone, without a team beside them. Too many new arrivals will alert the enemy. If we make any changes to the training program, it will raise alarms. We'll move the men in one or two at a time on the same rotation that the trainees are running right now."

"And when we get to the bottom of this?" Mason looked from the commander back to Mountain.

"Then the training can resume as usual," Doran stated.

Mason immediately churned through the names already popping up in his mind. How much could he tell his men? Obviously not much. Hell, he didn't know much himself. How much time did he have? "Timeline?"

The commander's final word told him of the urgency.

"Yesterday."

Find Magnus here!

To find out more visit Dale Mayer's website.

https://geni.us/DMSRMagnusUniversal

Author's Note

Thank you for reading Terkel's Twist: Terkel's Team, Book 8! If you enjoyed the book, please take a moment and leave a short review.

Dear reader,

I love to hear from readers, and you can contact me at my website: www.dalemayer.com or at my Facebook author page. To be informed of new releases and special offers, sign up for my newsletter or follow me on BookBub. And if you are interested in joining Dale Mayer's Reader Group, here is the Facebook sign up page.
http://geni.us/DaleMayerFBGroup

Cheers,
Dale Mayer

Get THREE Free Books Now!

Have you met the SEALS of Honor?

SEALs of Honor Books 1, 2, and 3. Follow the stories of brave, badass warriors who serve their country with honor and love their women to the limits of life and death.

Read Mason, Hawk, and Dane right now for FREE.

Go here and tell me where to send them!
https://dalemayer.com/masonfree

About the Author

Dale Mayer is a *USA Today* best-selling author, best known for her SEALs military romances, her Psychic Visions series, and her Lovely Lethal Garden cozy series. Her contemporary romances are raw and full of passion and emotion (Broken But ... Mending, Hathaway House series). Her thrillers will keep you guessing (Kate Morgan, By Death series), and her romantic comedies will keep you giggling (*It's a Dog's Life*, a stand-alone novella; and the Broken Protocols series, starring Charming Marvin, the cat).

Dale honors the stories that come to her—and some of them are crazy, break all the rules and cross multiple genres!

To go with her fiction, she also writes nonfiction in many different fields, with books available on résumé writing, companion gardening, and the US mortgage system. All her books are available in print and ebook format.

Connect with Dale Mayer Online

Dale's Website – www.dalemayer.com
Twitter – @DaleMayer
Facebook Page – geni.us/DaleMayerFBFanPage
Facebook Group – geni.us/DaleMayerFBGroup
BookBub – geni.us/DaleMayerBookbub
Instagram – geni.us/DaleMayerInstagram
Goodreads – geni.us/DaleMayerGoodreads
Newsletter – geni.us/DaleNews

Also by Dale Mayer

Published Adult Books:

Shadow Recon
Magnus, Book 1

Bullard's Battle
Ryland's Reach, Book 1
Cain's Cross, Book 2
Eton's Escape, Book 3
Garret's Gambit, Book 4
Kano's Keep, Book 5
Fallon's Flaw, Book 6
Quinn's Quest, Book 7
Bullard's Beauty, Book 8
Bullard's Best, Book 9
Bullard's Battle, Books 1–2
Bullard's Battle, Books 3–4
Bullard's Battle, Books 5–6
Bullard's Battle, Books 7–8

Terkel's Team
Damon's Deal, Book 1
Wade's War, Book 2
Gage's Goal, Book 3
Calum's Contact, Book 4
Rick's Road, Book 5

Scott's Summit, Book 6
Brody's Beast, Book 7
Terkel's Twist, Book 8
Terkel's Triumph, Book 9

Kate Morgan
Simon Says... Hide, Book 1
Simon Says... Jump, Book 2
Simon Says... Ride, Book 3
Simon Says... Scream, Book 4
Simon Says... Run, Book 5
Simon Says... Walk, Book 6

Hathaway House
Aaron, Book 1
Brock, Book 2
Cole, Book 3
Denton, Book 4
Elliot, Book 5
Finn, Book 6
Gregory, Book 7
Heath, Book 8
Iain, Book 9
Jaden, Book 10
Keith, Book 11
Lance, Book 12
Melissa, Book 13
Nash, Book 14
Owen, Book 15
Percy, Book 16
Quinton, Book 17
Ryatt, Book 18

Lovely Lethal Gardens

Arsenic in the Azaleas, Book 1

Bones in the Begonias, Book 2

Corpse in the Carnations, Book 3

Daggers in the Dahlias, Book 4

Evidence in the Echinacea, Book 5

Footprints in the Ferns, Book 6

Gun in the Gardenias, Book 7

Handcuffs in the Heather, Book 8

Ice Pick in the Ivy, Book 9

Jewels in the Juniper, Book 10

Killer in the Kiwis, Book 11

Lifeless in the Lilies, Book 12

Murder in the Marigolds, Book 13

Nabbed in the Nasturtiums, Book 14

Offed in the Orchids, Book 15

Poison in the Pansies, Book 16

Quarry in the Quince, Book 17

Revenge in the Roses, Book 18

Silenced in the Sunflowers, Book 19

Toes in the Tulips, Book 20

Lovely Lethal Gardens, Books 1–2

Lovely Lethal Gardens, Books 3–4

Lovely Lethal Gardens, Books 5–6

Lovely Lethal Gardens, Books 7–8

Lovely Lethal Gardens, Books 9–10

Psychic Vision Series

Tuesday's Child

Hide 'n Go Seek

Maddy's Floor

Garden of Sorrow

Knock Knock…
Rare Find
Eyes to the Soul
Now You See Her
Shattered
Into the Abyss
Seeds of Malice
Eye of the Falcon
Itsy-Bitsy Spider
Unmasked
Deep Beneath
From the Ashes
Stroke of Death
Ice Maiden
Snap, Crackle…
What If…
Talking Bones
String of Tears
Psychic Visions Books 1–3
Psychic Visions Books 4–6
Psychic Visions Books 7–9

By Death Series
Touched by Death
Haunted by Death
Chilled by Death
By Death Books 1–3

Broken Protocols – Romantic Comedy Series
Cat's Meow
Cat's Pajamas
Cat's Cradle

Cat's Claus
Broken Protocols 1-4

Broken and... Mending
Skin
Scars
Scales (of Justice)
Broken but... Mending 1-3

Glory
Genesis
Tori
Celeste
Glory Trilogy

Biker Blues
Morgan: Biker Blues, Volume 1
Cash: Biker Blues, Volume 2

SEALs of Honor
Mason: SEALs of Honor, Book 1
Hawk: SEALs of Honor, Book 2
Dane: SEALs of Honor, Book 3
Swede: SEALs of Honor, Book 4
Shadow: SEALs of Honor, Book 5
Cooper: SEALs of Honor, Book 6
Markus: SEALs of Honor, Book 7
Evan: SEALs of Honor, Book 8
Mason's Wish: SEALs of Honor, Book 9
Chase: SEALs of Honor, Book 10
Brett: SEALs of Honor, Book 11
Devlin: SEALs of Honor, Book 12
Easton: SEALs of Honor, Book 13

Ryder: SEALs of Honor, Book 14

Macklin: SEALs of Honor, Book 15

Corey: SEALs of Honor, Book 16

Warrick: SEALs of Honor, Book 17

Tanner: SEALs of Honor, Book 18

Jackson: SEALs of Honor, Book 19

Kanen: SEALs of Honor, Book 20

Nelson: SEALs of Honor, Book 21

Taylor: SEALs of Honor, Book 22

Colton: SEALs of Honor, Book 23

Troy: SEALs of Honor, Book 24

Axel: SEALs of Honor, Book 25

Baylor: SEALs of Honor, Book 26

Hudson: SEALs of Honor, Book 27

Lachlan: SEALs of Honor, Book 28

Paxton: SEALs of Honor, Book 29

Bronson: SEALs of Honor, Book 30

SEALs of Honor, Books 1–3

SEALs of Honor, Books 4–6

SEALs of Honor, Books 7–10

SEALs of Honor, Books 11–13

SEALs of Honor, Books 14–16

SEALs of Honor, Books 17–19

SEALs of Honor, Books 20–22

SEALs of Honor, Books 23–25

Heroes for Hire

Levi's Legend: Heroes for Hire, Book 1

Stone's Surrender: Heroes for Hire, Book 2

Merk's Mistake: Heroes for Hire, Book 3

Rhodes's Reward: Heroes for Hire, Book 4

Flynn's Firecracker: Heroes for Hire, Book 5

SEALs of Steel

Badger: SEALs of Steel, Book 1
Erick: SEALs of Steel, Book 2
Cade: SEALs of Steel, Book 3
Talon: SEALs of Steel, Book 4
Laszlo: SEALs of Steel, Book 5
Geir: SEALs of Steel, Book 6
Jager: SEALs of Steel, Book 7
The Final Reveal: SEALs of Steel, Book 8
SEALs of Steel, Books 1–4
SEALs of Steel, Books 5–8
SEALs of Steel, Books 1–8

The Mavericks

Kerrick, Book 1
Griffin, Book 2
Jax, Book 3
Beau, Book 4
Asher, Book 5
Ryker, Book 6
Miles, Book 7
Nico, Book 8
Keane, Book 9
Lennox, Book 10
Gavin, Book 11
Shane, Book 12
Diesel, Book 13
Jerricho, Book 14
Killian, Book 15
Hatch, Book 16
Corbin, Book 17
Aiden, Book 18

The Mavericks, Books 1–2
The Mavericks, Books 3–4
The Mavericks, Books 5–6
The Mavericks, Books 7–8
The Mavericks, Books 9–10
The Mavericks, Books 11–12

Collections
Dare to Be You…
Dare to Love…
Dare to be Strong…
RomanceX3

Standalone Novellas
It's a Dog's Life
Riana's Revenge
Second Chances

Published Young Adult Books:

Family Blood Ties Series
Vampire in Denial
Vampire in Distress
Vampire in Design
Vampire in Deceit
Vampire in Defiance
Vampire in Conflict
Vampire in Chaos
Vampire in Crisis
Vampire in Control
Vampire in Charge
Family Blood Ties Set 1–3

Family Blood Ties Set 1–5
Family Blood Ties Set 4–6
Family Blood Ties Set 7–9
Sian's Solution, A Family Blood Ties Series Prequel
   Novelette

Design series
Dangerous Designs
Deadly Designs
Darkest Designs
Design Series Trilogy

Standalone
In Cassie's Corner
Gem Stone (a Gemma Stone Mystery)
Time Thieves

Published Non-Fiction Books:

Career Essentials
Career Essentials: The Résumé
Career Essentials: The Cover Letter
Career Essentials: The Interview
Career Essentials: 3 in 1

Made in the USA
Coppell, TX
16 November 2022

86499934R00148